A Goat's Life

A Goat's Life

Bruce Shaffer

Goathouse Publishing books can be ordered through booksellers or at GoathousePublishing.com

ISBN 979-8-3303-7811-1

DEDICATION

In loving memory of our dear goats Tomás, Kevin, and Murphy who befriended me and my family for years.

ACKNOWLEDGEMENT

A special thanks to my wife Karen and sons Joel and Matt for taking the time to read and comment on the manuscript and maps. They're my loyal editors, and without them you'd be reading a lesser story.

Contents

REX RIVER VALLEY

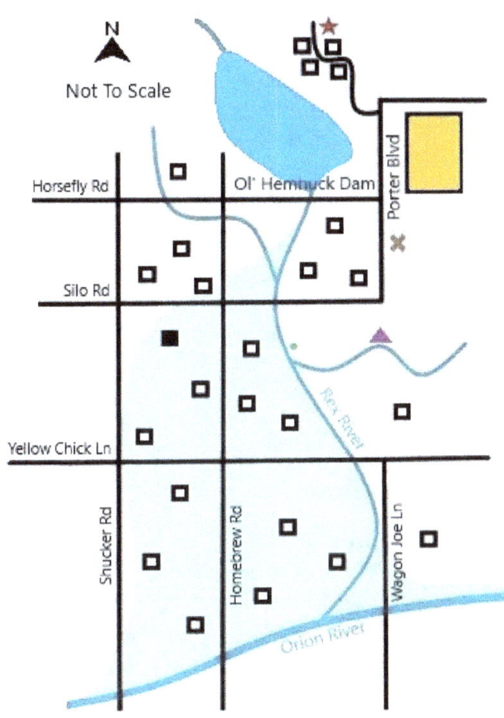

ORION RIVER

Homebrew Rd
Shucker Rd
Kidney Bean Island
N
Not To Scale
Gump Ave
Soccer Fields
Bailey Ave
Darbington
City
Limits
Estes Neighborhood
Lake April

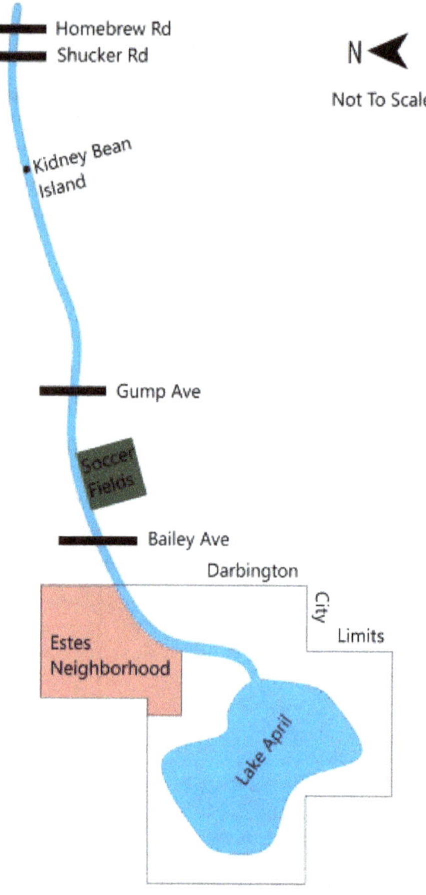

PART 1 — TALE OF TWO RANCHES

"Every man can tell how many goats or sheep he possesses, but not how many friends."
—*Marcus Tullius Cicero, Roman Statesman*

1

RODRIGUEZ RANCH

The brambles were bursting with blackberries, a phenomenon that didn't escape the dark brown eyes of little Juan Rodriguez. Unfortunately for him, at five years old he was unaware of the intricacies of berry picking, and the searing pain of a thorn prick sent him running to Mamá. "Owie!" he cried, tears streaming down his chubby rose-infused cheeks as he churned through the lush pasture at Rodriguez Ranch.

The hot August sun bore down on the 15-acre pasture, enclosed on all five sides by freshly painted white wooden fencing to form a giant home plate of sorts. The fence posts were plumb and rigid, the rails level and crack-free. If the pasture was home plate, its large oval pond was a home run.

The pond absorbed all the sun had to offer, enticing a flock of mallards to preen in the tepid water and splash about like children at play. Discharge from an inlet pipe splashed around more water, and the outlet pipe sucked it into a fence-line ditch. Orange crayfish shells, the remnants of egret and blue heron feedings, littered the shoreline. Wispy weeping willows shaded the pond perimeter, where a handful of western pond turtles lounged peacefully. It was a beautiful pond, on a gorgeous property in the stunning foothills above the Rex River Valley.

The rest of the pasture was dotted with smooth granite outcroppings and mature blue oak trees. The granite outcroppings were gray and sparkled with flecks of black crystals, the product of the slow cooling of magma deep within the earth millions of years ago. Some of the oak trees had gnarly branches from the ravages of time, and broken branches from gusty winds and the Rodriquez's goats nibbling on their lobed leaves, but those flaws just added to the uniqueness of the grandiose trees.

Tomás was but one of a dozen of the Rodriguez's goats. He stood on top of a granite boulder surveying the grounds, with nose in the air smelling watermelon, zucchini, and carrots blowing in the breeze from the neighbor's garden. He was a Nubian, with rabbit-like floppy ears, large almond-shaped eyes, a prominent Roman nose, mottled tan and white fur, long legs, and a short upward-pointing tail.

Smaller than the other Nubians, Tomás learned he must be cunning and assert himself to get what he wanted. And he wanted a lot— a healthy portion of grain at feeding time, an abundance of delectable blue oak leaves, a doe or two with whom he could have his way, a human caressing the crown of his head, and that neighbor's garden produce which always tickled his nose.

Suddenly little Juan Rodriguez, or JR as he was affectionately called, ran by crying and interrupted Tomás surveying from his perch on the granite boulder. *What now?* thought Tomás, *the little one's eyes leak water*, and he stepped down to investigate.

Just then JR reached Mamá who was reading a western in a nylon hammock strung between two of the mature blue oaks. "What's wrong baby?" she asked furrowing her brow.

"Owie!" cried JR again, shaking his bloody finger. Tomás watched as the human nuzzled her young, dried his eyes, and tended to his wound.

"It's alright honey," said Mamá, t-shirt wet with blotted tears and blue jeans stained with blotted blood. "Tell me what happened."

"The blackberry got me," said JR, the whimpering subsiding after a kiss from Mamá on his injured digit.

"Oh, poor baby. Your finger's all better now. We'll put a band-aid on it when we go in the house. We have to be very careful when we pick blackberries. They have sharp thorns. Let me show you how to pick 'em."

JR cracked a small smile. "Okay Mamá. Can we eat 'em too?"

"We can eat 'em too."

The humans nuzzled again and Tomás drew closer, curious about the show of affection. He followed them over to the blackberry brambles by the white wooden fencing, and soon his buddies joined him.

"What's going on?" bleated Rocky, who was the strongest of the goats. Why just yesterday he snapped a hefty willow branch to the ground by standing on his hind legs, reaching high and bending the branch down with his front legs, latching on to it with his vise-grip teeth, and shaking it violently. Some other goats quickly ran over to join Rocky nibbling on the tasty willow leaves of the downed branch.

"The humans are eating our berries," replied Tomás. Indeed, JR and Mamá smiled from the juicy sweetness of the blackberries, lips and fingertips tinged purple. "But don't worry, there's plenty for us."

"Plenty? The more they eat, the less we do."

Rocky was a Boer. The Boers, like the Nubians, were hornless at Rodriguez Ranch to keep them from harming each other. Unlike the Nubians, the Boers were stalky with thick legs and broad chests, and had white fur and brown heads.

The Boers numbered only four, a one-third minority, being less desirable than their milk-producing Nubian counterparts, but they weren't sold for meat like at most ranches. At Rodriguez Ranch the Boers enjoyed the good life of refugees, taken in from a shuttered ranch deemed inhumane, free from the blade of slaughter.

"Oh relax Rocky," bleated Gordie, a Nubian like Tomás, as he rolled onto his back pointing his legs straight up into the air as if he'd fainted. "Relax like me. I once saw a little guy do this after getting startled."

Gordie's sense of humor was legendary, but it was an acquired taste that not all of the goats appreciated. While Tomás wagged his tail in approval, Rocky did nothing. "Get a new act," he bleated. "You're embarrassing yourself."

Gordie righted himself and the trio started nibbling on the blackberries. They stood next to JR and Mamá and devoured not only the berries, but the woody stems, the leaves, and even the thorns too.

"Aren't they cute?" said Mamá. "Just look at their little mouths chew."

JR laughed and jumped up and down excitedly. "Can I feed 'em Mamá?"

"Of course you can," and she handed him a few berries. "Now hold your palm up like this and let them nibble from your hand."

Rocky quickly nudged over to accept the offering, wanting to minimize the humans' consumption of berries and maximize his. "Thanks little one," he bleated, and JR jumped up and down excitedly again, at twice the frequency of before.

After 15 minutes the goats had bared a patch of blackberry brambles and JR and Mamá had gotten their fill. "Bye goats," yelled JR, much of his face now a solid purple, and he left with Mamá for the house.

"Oh good, they're leaving," bleated Rocky, and he resumed eating.

After another 15 minutes of berry bliss Rocky, Tomás, and Gordie joined the other goats grazing on invasive weeds and plants throughout the pasture, avoiding the spray of several impulse sprinklers that chirped from atop white PVC risers. They ate star thistle, poison oak, mustard plant, spears of pampas grass, and some less appetizing fescue grass which a score of Suffolk sheep grazed.

"Good day sir," bleated one of the proper Suffolk ewes.

"Good day," replied Tomás.

"It's quite hot today. I certainly hope our dear humans can remove my fur soon."

"You look ridiculous," cracked Gordie, "like a big piece of cotton."

"How rude you are! Sometimes I wonder why we even try to talk with your kind."

A large Suffolk wether raised his head from the grass and came over, having overheard the conversation. "What's going on here ol' chap? My lady friend doesn't seem too happy with you."

"Just a joke gone bad," interjected Tomás. "He didn't mean anything by it."

"I certainly hope not. Do talk nice to the ladies, or next time I might have to butt you."

Rocky was also within earshot, and ran right up to the wether like a shell shot from a cannon. "You'll have to butt me first," he bleated, and he reared up on his hind legs.

The wether backed off. "Easy there, 'ol chap. No need for violence. We were just having a nice chat. We'll be on our way now. Come on lassie." The wether and ewe hurried away as Rocky dropped his front legs to the ground.

The grazing resumed without further incidents until suddenly a new circuit of impulse sprinklers engaged, sending goats and sheep scrambling, which startled more goats and sheep in a chain reaction of scrambling, until practically the whole pasture was in turmoil. It resembled kids in an Easter egg hunt, and when the sprinklers splashed three bee boxes in the corner of the pasture and roused their occupants, it was practically Armageddon.

"Hurry guys, follow me!" shouted Tomás, running to the corner of the pasture opposite the bee boxes. Gordie and Rocky were right behind, until they weren't. They circumnavigated a pair of Suffolks who were sprawled on the ground after colliding, and fell behind. "Come on guys!" shouted Tomás again.

Gordie and Rocky finally caught up with Tomás in the far corner of the pasture where all was quiet. They had outrun the bees, but some in the pasture weren't so lucky. "Look at that big piece of cotton hopping around like a rabbit," bleated Gordie between gulps of air.

"Maybe it's that fellow who threatened you," added Rocky.

"There's nothing we can do about it now," reasoned Tomás. "Let's eat."

So it was, another day of grazing at Rodriguez Ranch. Aside from the conflicts and calamities, whether perceived or real, the goats and sheep worked the pasture synergistically, keeping the grass and invasive weeds and plants down to the delight of the Rodriguez family, which would later reward them with a sundown feeding. The cherry on top, if you will, after a full day of grazing.

Evening came and it was time for milking. JR's Papá sat on a short three-legged wooden stool with a large sterile milk bucket tucked under the first of the six Nubian does at Rodriquez Ranch. Papá himself was tucked under the porch of a vast A-frame shed, shielded from the hot sun inching lower in the horizon. Inside the shed were the other does waiting their turn, resting comfortably on a clean dirt floor with access to a tub of fresh water, a salt lick block, and even some baking soda to help with their rumination.

Meanwhile Tomás, Gordie, Rocky, and the other Boers gathered around the porch like major leaguers around a batting cage. "Lookin' good!" shouted Rocky to the doe who was first up in the milk parade.

"Don't you guys have anything better to do?" she asked.

Turns out Tomás and Gordie did. With the left side of their abdomens bulging, they let out almost simultaneous burps. "Nice one," bleated Tomás.

"You too," replied Gordie.

Then they regurgitated their cuds back into their mouths for a second round of chewing and swallowing. "Second meal's my favorite, how 'bout you?" asked Tomás.

"I like fourth meal. The flavors seem more intense." And they regurgitated again.

Papá made sure the doe was happily eating from a bucket of grain and was secure in the goat stand before milking her. Then he grabbed each teat and rhythmically squeezed one teat and then the other.

"Nice teats!" shouted one of the Boers to the doe. She became agitated and stomped and Papá briefly lost his rhythm, but she settled down to deliver more milk. After five minutes the milk only trickled from the doe and the milk bucket was nearly full. She was done. Papá got a new milk bucket and the second doe. Tomás and Gordie regurgitated again.

"Hi Penny," bleated Tomás enthusiastically after swallowing his cud. Penny was his favorite doe, now in the goat stand. Sure, he'd had a go with the other does before, but Penny was the one he truly loved.

"Hi there. You know a girl could use a little privacy at a time like this. Why don't you and your buddies take a walk."

"But you're so cute when the human squirts you. We like to watch."

"Tomás!" Penny shot him the stink eye.

"Alright, we'll go," conceded Tomás. "Can I lie down by you tonight after the human gives us first meal?"

"I guess that would be okay."

"Good. See ya later. Stomp if the human squeezes too hard."

"Oh, I will." Tomás and Gordie regurgitated a final time, and then Rocky and the other Boers joined them for an evening stroll in the pasture.

Papá, having finished milking the last of the six Nubian does, cleaned up and had a wonderful chicken molé dinner with JR and Mamá. For dessert they dunked freshly baked chocolate chip cookies into cups of that fresh goat milk. "Yummy!" shouted JR with a milk mustache and a saturated cookie in his hand that was about to disintegrate.

"Your Mamá makes only the best," boasted Papá.

"Only the best for the best," gushed Mamá. They were a happy family and, almost to a fault, their lives were too perfect. Antonio Rodriguez, aka Papá, had the perfect job working as a software engineer for an upstart green energy company. His ability to work at home and flexible hours allowed him ample time for chores at the ranch.

One chore was selling all the goat kids born at the ranch. With six does and six horny bucks several kids were born each year, and the six lactating does produced enough milk to practically fill a swimming pool. The money earned from selling the kids and the excess milk went straight to the SPCA. The sheep were essentially lawnmowers for the pasture, with no lambs or lactating ewes to worry about since the males were wethers.

Manuela Rodriguez, aka Mamá, Antonio's wife of 10 years, left her perfect job teaching biology at a junior college to care full time for JR. And little JR was a kindergartner at the perfect parochial school, with a rigorous curriculum and only a mile down the road. Perfect. Everything was perfect.

"Thanks for dinner, honey. I'll go put the animals to bed now. And you . . ." Papá turned to JR and pointed, "I'll deal with you later." He tickled JR, who thrashed about laughing and dropped what was left of his cookie into his cup of milk.

Papá wheeled a large bag of grain in a wheelbarrow down to the pasture and, conditioned by his nightly trek, the goats and sheep stampeded to the A-frame shed as if drawn in by a magnet. They eagerly positioned themselves by a long wooden trough attached to the outside of the white wooden fencing by the shed. It was dusk, and a faint gibbous moon appeared over Rodriquez Ranch.

"Dinner time," declared Papá as he walked along the fence pouring grain into the trough. The goats and sheep poked their heads through the fence into the trough, pushing and shoving in a fierce feeding frenzy.

"Easy does it . . . lad . . . you're hurting me," bleated an elderly ewe to a young wether between bites of grain.

"Go lick yourself," he replied and shoved her aside.

"Penny, over here!" yelled Tomás, and she snuck in beside him.

"Oooh . . . so good . . . corn . . . oats . . . barley," she bleated between bites.

Gordie and Rocky formed a blockade of sorts, taking wide stances and sticking their butts out. When an aggressive wether tried to cut in, Rocky let him have it by butting him in the ribs. "I'd butt you too, but I don't want to make your face look any better!" shouted Gordie.

When the dust had settled, and it had literally— the ground by the A-frame shed was bare dirt, all of the livestock had eaten their fill, including Rogue the llama. Papá fed Rogue his own special bowl of hay and sliced apples in the shed while the goats and sheep fed at the trough.

Rogue was a beautiful creature with a majestic posture, soft brown and white wool, large banana-shaped ears, and a short bent tail. His behavior was another matter— a little too schizophrenic for Papá's liking. He could be affectionate, but at feeding time he could be impatient and rude.

Papá knew when Rogue made a shrill noise and laid back his ears, a pungent partly-digested grass offering would be hawked up and spit at his head with amazing accuracy. He countered by spraying water at Rogue from a bottle and, when the bottle was empty, throwing it at him with some choice four-letter words.

Despite his shortcomings, Rogue was the sentry. His job was to protect the goats and sheep from coyotes, mountain lions, and even wild dogs. He was to scare them away by making a startling alarm call that sounded like a rusty hinge, or by running, kicking, or spitting at them.

The gibbous moon was higher and brighter now, and all was quiet at Rodriguez Ranch. Rogue patrolled the pasture. Gordie and Rocky stood under the porch ruminating with some other goats and sheep and watching distant cars go by.

"Those animals with white eyes run one way," observed Gordie, "and those with red eyes run the other way."

"They make scary growling noises too," added Rocky. "I wouldn't want to have to butt one of them."

"Me neither. Could they be the makings of humans?"

"Could be. Humans make strange things."

"Yeah. I hate the sharp thing they make to cut our feet." Gordie and Rocky knelt down and regurgitated, chewed, and swallowed Papá's feeding again.

"I'm good for one more meal, then I think I'll call it a day," bleated Gordie.

Rocky burped. "Yeah, that sounds about right." They finished the next meal and laid down for the night.

Tomás and Penny laid down together in the A-frame shed for the goat's equivalent of pillow talk. "Want to have a go at it?" asked Tomás.

"Tomás! It's resting time. Just look at everyone else."

Tomás looked at the other prone goats and sheep in the shed. "I suppose you're right. Well then, want to lick me?"

"No."

"But I've seen you lick the humans. Why not me?"

"The humans' fur tastes like salt, yours doesn't."

"Oh . . . can you at least nuzzle me?"

"Of course I can."

They nuzzled for a minute and then Tomás burped. "Sorry, here comes another meal."

Penny drew back her head from Tomás and sighed. "Good night Tomás," she bleated.

*   *   *

Morning came. It was a busy time at Rodriguez Ranch and in the sky above. Papá came down to milk the six Nubian does again— leaving too much milk in their udders would cause them pain, then went back in the house for breakfast. The egrets and blue herons wanted breakfast too, and swooped down to the edge of the pond in search of crayfish, worms, and grasshoppers.

The sun rose higher above the horizon, positioning itself to radiate another hot August day over the foothills above the Rex River Valley. Commercial airplanes spewed contrails in the frigid high-altitude air, ferrying passengers to business meetings, vacations, and to life's other destinations. Billowy clouds drifted slowly eastward, morphing into recognizable objects if one had a vivid imagination.

"Mornin' Rocky."

"Mornin' Gordie."

Rocky tilted his head back. "Look at those birds up there. They make the scary growling noises too, and they leave white droppings that don't fall to the ground."

Gordie looked up. "I see big pieces of cotton . . . and they don't say annoying things like the ones we have here."

"Must be more makings of humans."

"Must be."

An hour later Papá came back to the pasture with JR and Mamá. He flipped up a metal latch that opened the pasture gate, and they walked to the hammock strung between two blue oaks. Tomás was watching.

"I'm gonna walk right through that white wood one day," bleated Tomás, "and get some carrots." He put his nose in the air. "That carrot smell is so strong, they can't be too far away."

"And how exactly are you gonna do that?" asked Penny.

"I've been watching the humans. They touch the shiny stick on top of the white wood and then walk right through."

"There's got to be more to it than that."

"I don't think so, but I'll keep watching. You can come along with me and we'll feast!"

"I'd like that."

The sheep grazed on the fescue in the pasture, avoiding the spray of the impulse sprinklers. Several pairs of goats, including Rocky and another Boer, reared up playfully to butt heads. It was the dance of the goats, a well-choreographed ritual.

"Hey you, gonna getcha good!" bleated Rocky to the other Boer.

"Just try it," the Boer replied. They reared up on their hind legs, cocked their heads, paused for a second to stare down each other, then dropped their front legs to the ground and rammed their hornless heads together. "Nice one. I'm impressed. Have a nice day," bleated the Boer and he walked away.

The sound of music came from the vicinity of the hammock. Papá sat on a smooth granite boulder, as he did once or twice a month, picking and strumming an acoustic guitar. He was a gifted guitarist and singer, performing *Dust in the Wind* for all to enjoy.

"I close my eyes, only for a moment and the moment's gone . . ."

Mamá sat in the hammock reading her western and tapping a foot to the music. JR was on the ground next to the hammock picking the grass before deciding to pick his nose. Though reading, Mamá had that third maternal eye which saw what JR was doing. "Stop that!" she shouted, and JR jerked his finger out of his nose.

While the sheep were skittish of the music, the goats were curious about it and many went to listen. They stood attentively around Papá in a crude semicircle, mesmerized by the different sounds.

"The human strokes hollow wood and howls like a dog," bleated Tomás to the group. "Do you like it?"

"I like it," bleated one.

"I hate dogs," bleated another.

"I want to eat the hollow wood," bleated yet another.

When Papá had finished singing some of the goats showed their appreciation by leaving droppings, others just walked away, but two of the Nubian does approached him, licked his hands, and presented their heads. "Anything for my ladies," said Papá as he caressed the crowns of their heads. It was the start of another perfect day at Rodriguez Ranch. Just perfect. Perhaps a little too perfect, and that was about to change.

2

JACKSON GOAT RANCH

Domino roamed the 10-acre field at Jackson Goat Ranch in the Rex River Valley. The field was parched and on gusty days the wind kicked up clouds of dust. The morning was calm and not yet hot, but in the afternoon with no trees in the field the only respite from the hot August sun was in the dilapidated goat barn.

The barn sheltered 60 Nubian, Boer, Savanna, and Spanish goats. Any goats not away on a vegetation management job sought shade in the barn on a dirt floor laden with droppings. Sometimes the goats were exposed to the sun below gaps in the corrugated metal roof panels. They drank from dirty tubs of water, with hay floating on top and weed seeds and dirt residue settled at the bottom. Their salt lick block was streaked with mucus and was seldom replaced.

A moving tuft of crabgrass caught Domino's eye. The border collie sprinted to the tuft and watched . . . and waited

. . . and waited some more. He froze with a paw in the air, his curved tail at attention, his body leaning forward and quivering with anticipation, and his nose inches off the ground. The tuft moved again and Domino was ready, pouncing and digging furiously until he found a tunneling gopher. In a flash he chomped on the gopher and snapped its neck, then shook it about like a ragdoll.

Several other gopher holes, both undisturbed and excavated by Domino, pocked the weed-infested field, which included star thistle, pepperweed, knapweed, Spanish broom, and crabgrass. Old wooden pallets also littered the field, including stacks of up to five high for the goats to climb on, which could be somewhat hazardous with nails poking out from some of the pallets.

"Domino!" shouted the dog's owner, Otis Jackson, and Domino took off running, tossing aside his ragdoll gopher and scattering any goats unfortunate enough to be in his way.

Otis Jackson was a string bean of a man— a shade over six-foot four and a shade under 160 pounds. He wore blue overalls and thrashed work boots with frayed shoe laces. His face was unshaven, had been for years, so a grayish-black beard sprouted from his chin to nearly his navel. The few hairs on his head were long and combed over, a futile attempt at concealing baldness.

If Otis was a string bean his younger twin brothers, Maynard and Cooper, were apples. The disparity between them became clear at dinner time. When they went out to a burger joint, which was quite frequently, Maynard and Cooper always "supersized" their triple bacon cheeseburger meals while Otis merely picked at a corn dog. When they ate at home, Maynard and Cooper always heaped mounds of food onto their plates while Otis struggled to clean his sparse plate of food. With full shoulder-length brown hair and clean-shaven faces, the disparity between Otis and the twins was even more pronounced.

Domino arrived at the feet of his master, panting and trembling with excitement. "Hello . . . yes . . . need something?" he barked.

"Good boy!" said Otis, and he tossed a punctured tennis ball with a ball launcher. It landed by 5-foot-high net-wire electric fencing which lacked tension and bent in and out like a slithering snake. Many of the PVC posts that supported the fence every 10 feet were crooked. Maintenance wasn't a priority or even fiscally possible sometimes at Jackson Goat Ranch, and to even have the ranch was somewhat of a miracle.

The Jackson brothers had done some hard time for a botched liquor store holdup. They charged in with baseball bats and demanded all the cash in the till and all the lottery tickets in the display case. The store clerk complied, and the brothers went out the door with 139 dollars and the potential for a lot more. The store clerk pulled out his shotgun and easily caught the fleeing brothers, who had the stamina of a sea cucumber. He ordered the brothers to the asphalt, and 10 minutes later they were taking a ride in a patrol car to the police station.

The brothers bounced around from job to job after being released from prison three years later. They tried washing dishes at fast-food restaurants, cleaning rooms at budget motels, and taking tickets at movie theaters. Then a phone call from a buddy Otis knew in prison changed everything. He told Otis about his farmhand job shoveling crap from horse stables, and that the farm owner had other openings. Between jobs at the time, Otis, Maynard, and Cooper jumped at the opportunity.

The farm owner had the brothers feed chickens, shear sheep, and trim goat hooves. Over time the farm owner gave them more responsibility with the goats; they not only trimmed their hooves but fed, dewormed, and brushed them. As a Christmas bonus one year the farm owner gave them their very own Boer goat. They took him home to their trailer and erected a makeshift wire fence to contain him.

It didn't. Several times the brothers had to recapture the head-butting goat with a rope and lots of sweat and swearing. When their mom passed away they inherited some money and, with good success breeding and some entrepreneurial luck, in four years they parlayed that one goat into 60.

Domino returned and dropped the ball at Otis' feet. "Oooh . . . do it again . . . do it again," he barked. Maynard and Cooper had joined Otis, rubbing their eyes and sipping their morning coffee. Otis launched the ball again.

"What's up today?" asked Maynard.

"We got a hay delivery comin' at eight," replied Otis. "Then we need to get out to that fire suppression job in Milton. I figure with thirty of the goats we can knock it out by the end of the day."

"Thirty huh," said Cooper, "I'll get a couple of trailers ready."

"Good. Make sure the pickups are gassed up."

"I will. When do you wanna get outta here?"

"Let's shoot for nine-thirty."

"Alright then. C'mon Maynard, let's go." The twins left but didn't get very far— Maynard faceplanted, and if not for some fancy footwork Cooper would have too.

"Goddamn gopher hole!" shouted Maynard. He slowly took inventory. Somehow his coffee cup was still in his hand but his coffee was percolating through the ground. A red scrape adorned his chin. Worst of all, his favorite pair of jeans had a massive rip in the crotch. He picked himself up and waddled off with Cooper. "Goddamn gopher hole!" he repeated.

Domino returned and dropped the ball at Otis' feet again. "Do it again," he barked, but this time Otis picked up the ball and pocketed it. "Do it again . . . huh . . . where is it?"

"Not this time boy, we've got work to do."

After the hay delivery, 30 of the Jacksons' goats climbed up two ramps leading to two goat trailers under the watchful eyes of Maynard and Cooper. Two by two the Nubians, Boers, Savannas, and Spanish goats went, like the animals boarding Noah's ark. The goats were strictly business commodities to the Jacksons, nothing more so they had no names, only numbers.

Tagged to the ear of one of the Spanish goats was the number 21. He slowly climbed up the ramp to the trailer that Maynard was towing. "For you, mi amigo," he bleated when

he reached the top of the ramp, and expelled some droppings.

The rift between Number 21 and Maynard was deep,
dating back to when Number 21 found a weak spot in the
fence when the electricity was off and escaped, only to find
the hood of Maynard's pickup truck. It was a good vantage
point to scout the unfamiliar territory, but it was short-lived
as the sound of denting metal had Maynard over there in a
flash.

If Maynard had his way, Number 21 would have been
sold for meat. But Otis and Cooper recognized that besides
his voracious appetite and impressive brush-clearing ability,
he was smart and could pull a cart. Having Number 21 lug
equipment around the ranch was invaluable.

Number 44, like Number 21, was a Spanish goat. She
slowly climbed up the ramp to the trailer that Cooper was
towing. Her long brown fur, large ears, and concaved face
were characteristic of the Spanish goats, but her extreme
underbite, small 70-pound frame, and wattles dangling
from each ear like earrings were not. She had horns like all
the goats at Jackson Goat Ranch, but hers were short devil
horns, inferior to the goats with long twisted horns.

"Move it along cow face," bleated Number 7 to Number
44.

"Yeah, move it along," bleated Number 14.

"Your ears are dragging on the ground," bleated Number
49.

"Lay off muchachos," replied Number 44, "or I'll let mis
amigas know who not to mate."

The hecklers looked at each other and then started stomping, which got the attention of Cooper. "Hey stop it! Stop it dumbass goats!" He stomped himself and soon the goat loading resumed without any further incidents.

Maynard and Cooper drove the goat trailers to Milton and Otis followed behind in his pickup truck. They arrived at a nice ranch house overrun with vegetation that encroached well into its 100-foot defensible space.

"Okay guys," said Otis, "the property owner has her panties in a wad over all this vegetation. The fire department is threatening to give her a citation and her insurance company is threatening to cancel her homeowner's policy. So here's the deal, let the goats eat everything out to a hundred feet except for the planted flowers and shrubs by the house. Cooper, you set up the fencing."

"Aye aye, captain."

"Maynard, you set up the water tubs and then help Cooper."

"Sure thing boss man."

"Then get the goats eatin' and put Domino to work. I'll be back at the end of the day to help you pack up. We gotta be done by dark."

Otis drove off and Cooper rolled out some net-wire electric fencing all the way around the ranch house, close to the planted flowers and shrubs to protect them from being eaten. Then he rolled out a much longer segment of fencing all the way around the house by the fenceless property boundary to contain any overzealous foragers.

Maynard joined Cooper to erect the fencing by pounding in PVC posts every 10 feet. When they were done, they energized the fencing and funneled the goats from the trailers into a roughly donut-shaped foraging area. It was full of wild rose, pine saplings, sage, vetch, French broom, coyote brush, and other ladder fuels that could convey fire into the canopies of the large sycamore trees that surrounded the house.

"Finally, we get first meal," bleated Number 21. "I was starting to wonder when the humans would let us out."

"I was getting hot in there," added Number 44.

The day was warming without a hint of a breeze. Domino panted and slobbered standing watch over his herd. "Enough talk," he barked, "and start eating. My human doesn't keep you to talk." He nipped at the goats' heals and they scattered and found leafy and woody delicacies to nibble, taking a break only for refreshing drinks from any of the three tubs of water.

Hours passed and the sun became high and hot, the vegetation short and sparse. Maynard and Cooper sat in folding chairs with their feet up on a couple of ice chests under the shade of an old sycamore tree, sipping beers and reading girly magazines. Suddenly, Domino spun and jumped and barked like a rabid dog. "Over here . . . hurry . . . over here!"

The twins got up as fast as they could, spilling their beers, and raced over to Domino. A group of goats stood by bleating agitatedly. It was Number 49, with his long twisted horns tangled in the electric fencing.

He thrashed about to no avail, becoming even more entangled and collapsing a small portion of the fencing. "Don't even think about it," barked Domino to the opportunistic goats.

"I'll cut the power!" yelled Maynard and he took off running. Cooper knelt by Number 49, and when the buzz of the fencing ceased he steadied the exhausted goat and cut away the tangled fencing with his hunting knife.

"Get outta here, dumbass goat!" yelled Cooper, and Number 49 took off running.

Maynard returned and saw the damage. "Shit. We gotta do a fuckin' patch job Coop."

Cooper sheathed his hunting knife. "No shit. Fuckin' dumbass goat!"

Number 49 took refuge under some gnawed coyote brush. A few other goats came over to get the gory details. "What happened?" asked Number 7.

"I saw blackberries beyond the shiny ropes," bleated Number 49, "and when I reached for them the ropes bit me. I should have known better. I was stuck until the human got me out. I don't feel so great now, I think I'll just lie here for a while."

"Let us know if there's anything we can do," bleated Number 14.

"Whose ears are dragging on the ground now?" shot Number 44 vengefully.

Number 14 reared up on his hind legs. "You can't talk to him like that!"

Number 21 reared up. "Let's give her a little leeway, it's been a long day for all of us." After a moment of consideration, the two bucks dropped their front legs to the ground and parted ways.

"Gracias for the support," bleated Number 44.

"De nada," answered Number 21.

"You're cute and you speak like me."

"Well, I'm speechless now." Number 21 paused for a moment, reached far back into his goat brain and bleated, "I like your ears."

If a goat can smile, Number 44 did— her extreme underbite appeared more prominent. "Gracias," she bleated. "I get teased about 'em too, but only by the weak." She rubbed against Number 21. "Want to join me for third meal?"

"Sure," and they regurgitated their cuds back into their mouths for a third round of chewing and swallowing.

Twilight approached and many of the goats stood around ruminating after a job well done. The donut-shaped area around the ranch house was denuded and wildfire-safe. Otis returned to help pack up the fencing and the water tubs, load the goats into the trailers, and to take care of a most important fiduciary task— collecting a hefty check from the little old lady who owned the property. "Thank you so much Mister Jackson," she said, "the yard looks great!"

"Glad to be of service, ma'am."

The Jacksons drove away at dusk, navigated the meandering drive back to their ranch, and released the goats back into the field. They settled into their dilapidated goat barn for the night, joining the 30 other goats who weren't needed in Milton.

Otis opened two screened windows in the barn to let in more breeze, which was pretty much nonexistent. Then he slammed shut the door. With their business commodities secure for the night, he headed back to the house to rest and get cleaned up for dinner.

It took Cooper a couple hours to prepare dinner. When it was ready, he and Maynard waited for Otis at the dinner table by playing a game of crazy eights. Otis sat down just as Maynard put the finishing touches on his victory. "Looooosseer!" he said, and made the "L" on his forehead with his thumb and index finger.

Cooper rolled his eyes. "Let's eat."

The brothers bowed their heads and observed a few seconds of silence. Then Otis drew a deep breath and recited, "Dear Lord, thank you for the food that graces our table, and we pray that you bless our goats and our business. Lastly, we pray that Maynard can buy a new pair of jeans that aren't too expensive. Amen."

"Amen," said Cooper.

Maynard wasn't amused. "Amen asshole."

The twins heaped huge piles of stew onto their plates, while Otis spooned his customary modest amount. Cooper doused his stew with a quarter bottle of ketchup, drawing unbelieving stares from his brothers, then they dug right in.

"Great stew Coop," said Otis.

"He wouldn't know with all that ketchup piled on," added Maynard.

"Meat's pretty tender, where'd ya get it?" asked Otis, now with a large spot of stew on his long grayish-black beard.

Cooper had a sheepish grin. "Right here at Jackson Goat Ranch. It's Number 49."

Otis was incredulous. "You slaughtered one of our own?"

"The electric fence had him half-baked anyway."

"That's right Otis," added Maynard. "Poor bastard wasn't himself after getting caught in the fence. Domino was a good boy and tried to get him goin', but the dumbass just moved to another bush and set 'er down." Domino sat at attention at Maynard's feet, stringers dangling from both sides of his mouth, eyes intent on the prize. "Ain't that right Domino, you were a good boy. Yes you were," and Maynard dropped a chunk of Number 49 to the floor which Domino instantly gobbled up.

"Well, I can't say I condone what you did," concluded Otis. "This is a pretty costly meal . . . but it sure tastes so damn good!"

After dinner the brothers parked in front of the television to watch a movie. Soon they were all snoring after a hard day's work. Johnny Cash's *Folsom Prison Blues* rang out and interrupted their slumber, and Otis answered his phone. "Hello . . . uh huh . . . really . . . uh huh . . . why thank you sir . . . that's great news . . . you won't be disappointed . . . next Monday's perfect . . . okay . . . thank you again . . . talk to you soon . . . bye."

Otis erupted when he got off the phone. "Hallelujah! Thank you Jesus! I just got a call from Sam down at the flood control agency. Says we got the levee maintenance contract next spring. We gotta get the grass and weeds down so the water flows better, and expose rodent holes for them to fill. And we'll do it without firin' up a weed eater and pollutin' the air, or sprayin' any poison. Those fuckin' bureaucrats just love us!"

PART 2 — OL' HEMHUCK

"Never give up; for even rivers someday wash dams away."
—*Arthur Golden, American Author*

3

BUILDING A DREAM

The farmers in the arid Rex River Valley had a dream—to have an abundant water supply to irrigate their crops. When the Great Depression hit, to kickstart the economy the federal government helped fund the construction of many public works projects. The farmers banded together with state and local government officials to get a piece of the pie, and with it they built more than a dam, they built a dream.

The dam was named for Alfred Hemhuck, the late state senator who was instrumental in securing federal funds, and it was affectionately known as Ol' Hemhuck. Dam construction started in the summer of 1934 and finished two years later, and then on September 12, 1936 a dedication ceremony was held.

It was a glorious morning. Hundreds of local residents, many of whom were farmers, crowded the one-lane gravel road across the crest of Ol' Hemhuck. The local high school marching band stood by ready to play. Large nets held hundreds of red, white, and blue helium balloons at each end of the dam. The uniformed color guard stood at attention holding rifles and the American and California flags. Five dignitaries in suits stood by with an oversized pair of scissors ready to cut a red ribbon stretched taut across the dam crest road. A sixth dignitary, Andrew Hemhuck, an up-and-coming politician and the son of Alfred, stood poised at a podium adjusting the microphone and then he spoke:

"Good morning everyone and welcome to the dedication ceremony for Ol' Hemhuck. I know my dad would be tickled to see this huge crowd, this engineering marvel below our feet, and of course that beautiful lake water pooling behind it. Though the lake isn't full just yet, when it is it'll have a capacity of forty-eight thousand acre-feet, enough to keep our farmers quite happy; and our recreational boaters, fishermen, and swimmers too."

A flock of seagulls squawked over the lake, and a gaggle of geese turned on final approach to splashdown on the calm azure water. Fishermen in motorboats, row boats, and even in canoes held their lines in the water, and the planted rainbow trout below eyed their appetizing lures.

"Now for some nerdy facts that I just have to give you. Our engineers selected this narrow section of the Rex River for Ol' Hemhuck to minimize the construction cost, which ended up being one point nine million dollars. With great gratitude to our friends in Washington, the federal government paid over seventy percent of the cost."

"She's made of seven-hundred ninety-thousand cubic yards of dirt and rock, put together indestructibly with the brains of our engineers and the skills of our construction workers. With an impervious clay core, compacted layers of soil, and rock slope protection, this monolith is here to stay and serve you for years to come."

"Are you bored yet?" asked Andrew, and the crowd chuckled. "Just a few more facts and then we can start the celebration. Ol' Hemhuck collects runoff from an eighty-two-square-mile drainage area. A lot of water can come in here, which is what we want, but if too much is comin' in then the concrete spillway will send the excess water down the river and keep Ol' Hemhuck safe. Normally, and this is the best part, only her three gated outlets will release the water to our great farmers to grow their crops and support our regional economy." The crowd cheered, including many farmers who also hugged and slapped each other's backs.

"Finally, I'd like to thank all of our partners in this great endeavor— the state, federal, and local government officials; the engineers, hydrologists, and draftsmen; the contractors, project managers, and skilled tradesmen; and of course you, the community, and any others I may have forgotten to mention. Now, without further ado, let's countdown from five and celebrate! Ready? Five, four, three, two, one!"

The crowd roared as the five dignitaries cut the red ribbon stretched across the dam crest road, and one of the color guard members released the red, white, and blue helium balloons which drifted upwards to color the sky. Then the color guard raised the American and California flags and the marching band played the national anthem. Nearly everyone placed their right hands on their hearts and sent a loud chorus of song throughout the Rex River Valley.

On the lake surface a fisherman fought with a large rainbow trout, one hand pulling hard on the rod and the other cranking frantically on the reel. Deep below the lake surface the greatest hydrostatic forces pressed against Ol' Hemhuck, where some defective soil compaction around the three outlet conduits went undetected.

4

WATER WAR

Ol' Humhuck performed well over the years since that wonderful dedication day in 1936. It passed floodwaters without any major problems to the dam itself, and without flooding downstream crops and residences. Sure, large sediment loads from floodwaters had to be dredged from the lake periodically, and washed-up trees and branches had to be removed from the lake and shoreline, but they were to be expected and always were included in the annual maintenance budget. The scariest moment was during the 1964 flood when one of the outlet gates jammed briefly at 1/4 open, but with some extra lubricating grease the dam operator got it all the way open and Ol' Hemhuck was never in danger.

During most years Ol' Hemhuck supplied the farmers with nourishing irrigation water for their crops without compromising lake levels and the boating, fishing, and swimming that happened there. However, during drought years some farmers had to take less than a full share of their water right, the worst of which was in 1999 when they took as little as 1/4 share and their crop production and pocketbooks suffered significantly. Another severe drought was inevitable, but what wasn't inevitable or even remotely predictable was the fury of the water war after Jerry Whitney came to town.

Jerry was a big jovial guy. If he had a long white beard he might even pass for Santa Claus. But he had no beard and, due to an extramarital affair, he had no wife either. She kicked him out of the house so he packed up his bags, moved out west, and bought the old Miller property right next door to Cecil Robinson.

"Howdy neighbor," said Cecil, extending a cold beer out to Jerry. "Welcome to the neighborhood."

Jerry set down the box he was carrying into his new house and grabbed the beer. "Why thank you. That's so nice . . . "

"Cecil. Cecil Robinson."

"I'm Jerry Whitney, pleased to meet you," and they shared a firm handshake.

"What brings you out here?"

"Thought I'd try my luck at farming. Back at my Kansas farm I was having a tough go of it. That and my wife gave me the boot."

"Oh, I'm sorry to hear that. You know it'll be tough here too, but at least we've got plenty of water for the crops. Well, most of the time."

"That's good to hear. I have a sense of the water situation from my real estate agent, but if you don't mind can I ask you some questions about it?"

"Fire away."

"I know that we pump from the river, but the water rights are a little confusing to me. Is it true that I get half the water that you get?"

"Yeah, roughly half. That's because your acreage is roughly half the acreage of mine."

"Hmmm . . . okay. Damn regulations. I've never been one for regulations. Can't get anything done with 'em if you ask me."

"That's the way it works around here. Been that way for decades."

"What if someone decides to take a bigger drink, so to speak?"

"Yeah, that's happened a few times over the years. We fine 'em . . . if we catch 'em. We're on the honor system here so no one's actively patrolling."

"Good to know. Alright then, thanks for the beer." Jerry picked up the box and headed for his house. "I'll see ya around."

"See ya around."

Jerry's and Cecil's crops thrived that year— lettuce and broccoli in the winter, and corn, tomato, and almonds in the summer. Almonds were the cash crop that put their financial ledgers in the black, which was great for Cecil but was absolutely essential for Jerry, who had financial obligations for two mortgages and alimony. And then a severe drought hit the next year, and Jerry wasn't so jovial anymore.

"Just a minute," said Cecil as he rushed to answer the knock on his front door.

"Hey there," said Jerry when the door opened, and he held up a paper. "Did you get one of these?"

Cecil moved in close to the paper and squinted. "Sure did. That's the notice we get from Ol' Hemhuck Water District during dry years."

"Says here that junior water users will get as little as a quarter share of our water right this year. Am I a junior water user?"

"Afraid so. My family's had this property over a hundred years, since before Ol' Hemhuck, so I'm a senior water user. You have the property Miller developed in the nineteen sixties, so you're a junior water user."

"Well that's just fuckin' great. So you're tellin' me I'll get a quarter of what I got last year, which is already half of what you got because of my smaller property?"

"More or less."

"That's bullshit! I got crops to grow and bills to pay."

"I'm sorry."

"Wait a minute, if you get so much water how 'bout you sell me some of yours?"

"Sorry, can't do that. I got my own bills to pay."

"Well then what can I do?"

"I hate to say it, but you might consider fallowing some of your land."

"Bullshit!" said Jerry, "and fuck you Robinson!" he added as he walked out the door. Thus began an intense feud rivaling that of the Hatfields and McCoys.

A couple weeks later Cecil's rottweiler, Brutus, awakened him with frenzied barking around 3 a.m. Cecil rubbed his eyes. "What is it boy?" he mumbled, and then heard the distant sound of a pump motor through his cracked-open bedroom window. "Well I'll be damned. That crazy fool," he said to himself and then went back to bed.

In the morning Cecil and a growling Brutus approached Jerry who was shoveling some dirt. "I heard you pumping overnight after pumping twice earlier this week. Didn't you think I'd hear you? What the hell are you doin'?"

"Gotta water my crops."

"Yeah? Well you gotta play by the rules too. I used to have an occasional beer with Miller down by the river. I've seen your pump and pipe. You got a twenty-horsepower pump and a four-inch pipe, same setup as me. I got my drought watering schedule from the district. Says I can water five times a month for eight hours each time. I sure as hell know your schedule calls for a lot less with your smaller property and with you being a junior water user. I'll be watchin' you."

"Don't look to hard. Bad things might happen."

"Is that a threat?"

"What do you think?"

"I think you better shape up Whitney," and both men and growling dog stomped off.

The next day Jerry was at it again, pumping and irrigating and pissing off Cecil, who decided to take a trip down to the Ol' Hemhuck Water District office. He brought back with him a boyish-looking worker wearing shorts and a skewed ballcap and chewing on a wad of gum. They confronted Jerry.

"Excuse me sir," said the worker. Jerry looked up from a machete he was sharpening. "Cecil here says you've been overwatering. Any truth to that?"

"Absolutely not. There must be some misunderstanding."

"Lier!" shouted Cecil.

"Alright, easy now," said the worker. "I see that you're watering today. We're in a drought you know, and your schedule says you can water only once a month. So today is it. I don't want to see you watering the rest of the month. Consider this a warning. Next time you get a thousand dollar fine."

"You have nothing to worry about."

"Alright then, have a nice day," and Cecil and the worker stepped away.

All was quiet the next few days, but then Cecil noticed two rows of his young tomato plants were dying. He suspected foul play, as his other 10 rows of tomatoes were just fine. Cecil examined a plant and saw no aphids, just shriveled brown leaves. A shiver coursed through his body when he saw an empty herbicide jug, knowing that Jerry had intentionally left it as a hostile message.

Cecil thought long and hard about how to respond. *Spray the hell out of Jerry's tomatoes with herbicide? Maybe. Send a brick through his living room window? Oh, the look on his face! No, I need to do something more permanent, more practical.*

A few nights later around 3 a.m., Brutus again awakened Cecil with frenzied barking. Cecil rubbed his eyes and smiled. Through his cracked-open bedroom window he heard the distant sound of Jerry's pump motor, and also the sound of Jerry's mouth spewing a long series of loud obscenities into the night air. Cecil went back to bed quite content, and imagined the scenario over at Jerry's pump.

Having drilled several holes into the pump discharge pipe, Cecil imagined water going everywhere. And having poured some quickset concrete over the connection between the pump and the discharge pipe, he knew removing the damaged pipe would be quite difficult.

It was getting ugly, and Cecil was on high alert. Every time Brutus barked, which was quite often with squirrels climbing up trees and birds flying overhead, his stomach knotted. The day passed rather quickly after Cecil fell asleep on the sofa watching a movie on television. The evening was relaxed and quiet without Brutus' incessant yapping. *A little too quiet,* thought Cecil. *Where's Brutus?*

Cecil traversed his property in search of his good boy. For 30 minutes he searched, calling out to Brutus many times, looking in his three outbuildings, and even checking in the cab of his pickup truck parked out front. He had one more place to look. The knot in his stomach returned.

Down on the bank of the Rex River, Cecil walked slowly on the sloped ground until he saw two buzzards picking at a meal. Then he ran. The buzzards flew away to reveal his beloved Brutus with an arrow through his heart. He read a note attached to the shaft of the arrow, "Don't mess with me!"

Cecil sat down and sobbed uncontrollably for a few moments, and stroked his fallen friend. Then he carried Brutus back into the garage, gently laid him down, pulled out the arrow, and placed a sheet over him. He wiped the last of his tears away and proclaimed, "I'm gonna kill that fucker!" and he marched to his gun cabinet.

The gun cabinet was unlocked and the rifles were loaded. Cecil grabbed his favorite one and bounded over to Jerry's house. He walked slower now, down the gravel path leading to the front door, and mustered up his courage. His heart pounded as he eased the rifle onto his shoulder and advanced. And then he was suddenly on his back staring at the sky.

The pain in his neck was overwhelming and breathing was difficult. Instinctively Cecil touched his neck and felt around. *Damn, that's blood*, he thought. *But what's this? No, it can't be. Shit, it must be. The fucker got me with an arrow. Can't move. Can't breathe. This could be bad. Feelin' kinda woozy. Birds in the sky. Brutus always barked at birds in the . . . "*

* * *

The tragic news about Cecil spread like wildfire throughout the farming community, and Jerry was on the run. An emergency meeting of the Ol' Hemhuck Water District Board of Directors was held at their office two days later. The five members of the board were old white men, the oldest of which was Robert Sutton, President of the Board. He called the meeting to order and spoke from his chair at a big round table:

"Thank you everyone for attending today, especially under such dire circumstances. We've lost one of our long-time customers, Cecil Robinson. I know that to many of us he was more than a customer, he was a friend. We're here today to vote on a proposal that would help ensure that another needless killing of a district customer never happens again. I understand that we sent one of our field workers over to Cecil's property to mediate a dispute with his neighbor, the presumed killer, but that wasn't enough."

Robert sipped from a glass of water and continued. "I'd like to propose that we install meters on every pump discharge pipe in the district to measure the volume of water being used. We can check the meters remotely for compliance with the customers' approved watering schedules. Any non-compliance would be dealt with a warning first, and then a fine or fines, as we do now. The meters would do the policing for us so customers don't have to, and that might just prevent more bloodshed."

"We have a young engineer here today to point out an alternative proposal, one nothing to do with water meters, for an entirely different purpose. Megan Riley, please go ahead."

Megan sat directly across from Robert at the big round table. She was a diminutive woman, but her career ambitions were huge. After graduating near the top of her class two years ago, she already had important job responsibilities at Ol' Hemhuck Water District. She had glasses and long brown hair, and wore a nice gray business suit with matching gray low-heel pumps. She cleared her throat and spoke to the old men:

"Good morning gentlemen. Before you vote on the water metering expenditure, I wanted to alert you to an issue I think is even more critical. I've been performing quarterly inspections of Ol' Hemhuck and have noticed some concerning seepage by the outlets."

"Are you sure it's seepage?" asked Robert.

Megan withheld her irritation with the question. "Absolutely. While some seepage under the dam is normal, the seepage I'm seeing isn't normal. It's greater than before and the water has a touch of brown, which could mean that some soil is being carried away."

"It's probably just some turbid lake water coming out of the outlets."

Again she withheld her irritation. "I know the difference between seepage and outlet flow, sir. I'm very concerned the seepage will get worse and lead to catastrophic dam failure."

"That's hogwash young lady, if you'll pardon the expression."

"I don't think so, and I think it's essential that we act on my observations. I'd like to get our geotechnical engineers to do some exploratory drilling by the outlet conduits."

"That would cost a fortune."

"Which gets us to the point of this meeting. I know our maintenance budget is limited, but I think it's absolutely necessary that we use some of it for the drilling, and not use any of it for the water metering. Can't we use our capital improvement fund for the metering?"

"No, it's already earmarked for a new boat ramp and marina."

"Can't the customers pay for the meters?"

"The proposal is that they pay for half, any more isn't fair. They're expensive little buggers, about two-thousand dollars a shot." Robert took another sip of water. "Alright, I think we've heard enough. I'd like to remind the board that we have a deceased customer because of our inability to quell a dispute, and we expect water metering to eliminate customer disputes. Okay, let's vote."

They went around the table with verbal "ayes" and "nays." When they had finished the count was five to zero, in favor of installing water meters. "Okay, it's settled then," said Robert. "We'll use funds from the maintenance budget to install meters on every pump discharge pipe in the district. And young lady, keep an eye on that seepage or whatever it is. Next year's maintenance budget might be able to address it."

"But sir, I implore you. The safety of residents in the Rex River Valley is at risk!"

"Keep an eye on it. That will be all."

"But sir—"

"This meeting is adjourned!"

PART 3 — INTO THE FRAY

"The best of men have ever loved repose. They hate to mingle in the filthy fray; where the soul sours, and gradual rancour grows, imbitter'd more from peevish day to day."

—*James Thomson, Scottish Poet*

5

THE COYOTES SING

Rogue patrolled the still pasture at Rodriguez Ranch on a crisp spring night under a full moon. Papá had fed the goats and sheep their usual grain for dinner, and they laid in the A-frame shed and under its porch ruminating with bloated abdomens. Gordie and Rocky watched the distant cars go by from the porch, as they did every night.

"Just once I'd like to see the animals with white eyes and the animals with red eyes change directions," observed Gordie.

"I'd like them to be quiet and stop making those growling noises," added Rocky.

Tomás and Penny, had they been human, were as good as married and spent another night lying down together in the A-frame shed.

"Want to have a go at it?" Tomás' question was as much of a reflex as regurgitating and chewing his cud.

"We already had a go at it today, remember?"

"Oh yeah. You were wonderful. How was I?"

"Efficient."

"Want to have a go at it tomorrow?"

"Tomás, it's resting time! We'll have that discussion tomorrow."

A group of sheep huddled together under the porch next to Gordie and Rocky, their huffing in the cool air producing a small cloud. One of the wethers was bleating a bedtime story:

"This is a story I'm sure your mums and dads have told you, and before that their mums and dads told them. I like to tell it too and I hope you enjoy it. There was a hilly pasture that had no white wood and everyone could eat wherever they wanted. A human held a long stick and he had a dog to watch closely over everyone. They became distracted when light flashed in the sky and the sky yelled at them. The loud sky frightened a young lass who ran away and disappeared from the end of the pasture. The others followed her and also disappeared. When the human and the dog came to the end of the pasture they looked far down and saw that everyone was free and sleeping in the rocks by the water. The human used his long stick and the dog yelled to stop the others from disappearing, and they had to go to a pasture with white wood where they would never be free."

The other sheep looked around at each other and then back to the wether. "The point of the story," the wether continued, "is we must always follow each other, and one day we may become free and sleep as we choose." The other sheep looked around at each other and nodded in agreement.

Then the sheep became very still. "What's that noise?" asked one of them.

"It's the human howling like a dog," bleated another.

"Now? Not when it's time for us to rest."

"Then what was it?"

The sheep listened some more and all was quiet until a somewhat familiar noise that sounded like a rusty hinge broke the silence. It was Rogue's alarm call, and it most definitely woke up those who were sleeping. Rogue bravely fended off a pack of eight coyotes with his kicking and spitting, but soon he was overwhelmed and they got through his defenses. It became mealtime.

Tomás got up hastily with Penny and ran about yelling, "It's dogs! It's dogs!" Gordie and Rocky and the rest of the goats sprang to their hooves and joined Tomás.

"Follow each other!" yelled the storytelling wether, and the sheep frantically assembled and ran together randomly through the pasture.

"No wait! Follow me! Everyone follow me!" yelled Tomás to the sheep, but it was too late and four of the ravenous coyotes attacked an elderly ewe who was just a little slower than the rest of the flock. They knocked her onto her back and she was helpless, unable to get up or fight. The ewe kicked and bleated wildly, but the coyotes latched on to her throat and soon it was quiet again.

The evisceration was methodical and quick, the eating bloody and gluttonous. The other four coyotes took down a second ewe and eviscerated and ate. They joined the rest of the pack in sending out chilling high-pitched yips and yowls into the night air, warning other animals to stay away from their prey.

"This way! Quickly!" yelled Tomás, and the other goats and a few spooked sheep ran behind him to the pasture gate.

"Now what? Where do we go?" asked a frightened Penny.

"I told you we'd walk right through the white wood one day," reassured Tomás. "Now is the time." He put his front hooves on the middle rail of the gate, and raised his face to the top of the gate. With his nose Tomás frantically poked and jostled the metal gate latch, but the gate remained closed.

"Hurry Tomás!" yelled a panicked nubian doe.

"Let me try," bleated Rocky, and he assumed the same position Tomás had on the gate just a moment ago. Rocky was the strongest of the goats, but in this situation that did him no good. His nose did him good, however, when the gate latch miraculously clicked after a few swipes. Rocky was a big Boer, and with his body leaning forward on his front legs the gate easily pushed open.

"Hurry, everybody through," he bleated as he held the gate open.

"Thank you," bleated Gordie as he passed through the gate. For one of the few times in his life he was serious, no bleating of a clever quip, only sincere appreciation.

Tomás was the last one through the gate and echoed Gordie's sentiment. "Thanks Rocky," he bleated, and gently butted his buddy. The runaways numbered 15, 12 goats and three sheep, and they ran for their lives into the darkness without a clue in the world of where to go.

Papá was slow to respond to the uproar, having been caught off guard in the bathtub. He ran down to the pasture in only his robe, shined a bright flashlight, and surveyed the battlefield. He saw Rogue lying down and chewing his cud by the bee boxes in the corner of the pasture. The mighty Rogue had fought the good fight but knew his limitations and, without any real bonds with any of the goats and sheep, he was content to watch the massacre unfold.

The beam of Papá's flashlight caught a white fuzzy mass against the green of the pasture, and with a clockwise sweep it caught a second one. The two dead sheep alarmed Papá, but even more alarming was that the gate was open. "Shit," he said to himself, a rare outburst of profanity but definitely called for in this situation. "Those clever goats."

Papá immediately shut the gate and looked for any sign that the coyotes were still in the pasture. He carefully approached what was left of each sheep carcass and concluded that the coyotes had gotten their fill and left the premises. His last task before returning to the bathtub and rejuvenating it with hot water was doing a quick livestock head count. He counted only three agitated sheep hanging out by the A-frame shed, but a full scan of his 15 acres in the morning light revealed 12 more . . . but no goats.

Papá was sad that he couldn't milk his Nubian does anymore, or play guitar and sing to his curious goats, or stroke the soft furry heads of his demanding goats, or get licked by his affectionate goats. Yes, Papá would miss all of that, for those goats were on a journey to nowhere.

6

JOURNEY TO NOWHERE

Once clear of the pasture, the herd ran down the asphalt driveway at Rodriguez Ranch. The clippety-clop of 60 hooves meeting road was noisy but not enough to trigger any action from the Rodriguez's neighbors. The herd regrouped at the end of the driveway to figure out its next move. "I don't like the hard black grass," bleated a Boer. "We should go back."

"Not so fast," bleated Tomás. "You saw what happened back there. We must keep going. Does everybody agree?"

"We'll follow you," bleated one of the sheep.

"You'd follow a gopher to its hole," quipped Gordie.

"We'll need food in the morning," noted Rocky. "Take us to it."

Tomás put his nose in the air. "How 'bout some food right now? This way." They hung a left onto the paved private road serving five houses, including the Rodriguez's house at the end of the road, and clippety-clopped down the road. Tomás suddenly stopped when they reached the first house on the road. "Come with me everyone," he bleated.

"Where are we going?" asked a Boer.

"Peas and asparagus are just over there. Anybody want some?" Without delay they headed for a large raised-bed garden. Unbeknownst to them, two women were sipping steamy hot drinks on the deck of the house which over-looked the garden. The women easily spotted them, ran into the house, and came back each clanging a pot with a spoon.

"Let's get outta here," bleated Tomás. "The sky is loud," and they quickly retreated back to the road. Tomás was dis-appointed. "One day we'll feast here, but now isn't the time. We must go further and we'll find food in the morning."

The private road snaked and dropped 150 feet in the next quarter mile until it ended at Porter Boulevard, a two-lane country thoroughfare. Rush hour had passed but a steady stream of cars still whizzed by. The herd approached with caution. "It's the growling animals with white eyes and red eyes," bleated Rocky.

Gordie tucked his tail between his legs. "I don't like them. They're much bigger and faster than I imagined. They must be the makings of humans." The herd got closer, a little too close, and a passing motorist honked. The loud horn blow startled everyone even more than Rogue's alarm call did, and one of the Nubian does panicked and took off run-ning across Porter Boulevard, followed closely by a Suffolk wether.

It was a lethal game of *Frogger,* culminating in the screeching of tires, the clanging of metal, and the shattering of glass. A young man extracted himself from the deployed airbag of a mangled car and staggered out. The other cars on Porter Boulevard came to an abrupt stop, and one of the drivers lit a flare. Penny glimpsed the red asphalt and the coyote-like mutilation of her pasture mates. It was overwhelming and she pressed her head against a mile marker. Tomás quickly found Penny and nuzzled her. "I'm sorry," he bleated. "Did you know them?"

"I knew her. We'd talk when the human squirted us. Her name was Pearl and she loved to climb on the rocks."

Rocky backed far away from the mangled car and the dazed driver. "We need to go NOW," he bleated. "That animal with white eyes is mean like the dogs we escaped from, and that human who rode it is no better."

Tomás surveyed the accident scene. "Rocky's right. This is no place for us." With the traffic stopped, they ran across Porter Boulevard into an open field. It was unmaintained and contained the usual invasive weeds and plants— star thistle, mustard plant, pepperweed, knapweed, and Spanish broom. They kept running through the field without stopping to graze, still spooked from losing two of their own. The field abruptly ended at the parking lot of the county fairgrounds where 4-H events, rodeos, and of course the county fair were held.

"Oh no, more hard black grass!" bleated a Nubian doe. "I don't like it."

"Yeah, we don't like it," bleated another doe.

Tomás thought for a moment. "Alright, let's go this way," and they veered right, more or less paralleling Porter Boulevard, and traversed the weedy field. They came to a welcome grove of mature blue oak trees and thought of home.

The thought quickly evaporated. "Why looky here at the cute little animals," said a bearded homeless man to his three buddies. They sat on inverted plastic buckets by a roaring fire, the smoke and embers drifting up through the grand oak branches. Trash littered the grove— baked bean cans, cereal boxes, sandwich wrappers, pie tins, used paper towels and worse, used toilet paper; you name it, it was there.

Empty bottles of booze were there . . . in force, and the homeless men were drunk. They were smelly and dirty; but with tattered down jackets, wool beanies, and the roaring fire they were warm and happy. The herd was not happy with their human neighbors, however, and they kept their distance.

"Are those goats and sheep?" mused the bearded man. "Jeb, get your hunting knife, and go get us some pork chops." Jeb unsheathed his knife, stood up, and promptly fell down, the result of a few too many.

"Is it safe to stay here overnight?" asked Penny. "The humans seem harmless, and the trees remind me of home. Let's stay."

Tomás and the others agreed. "If the humans get too close we can leave," he bleated.

"Jeb, you fuckin' idiot," said the bearded man. "Am I gonna have to show you how to do it? Gimme that thing," and he grabbed the knife . . . blade end first. "Goddamn it Jeb! You stuck me!" He sucked his wound for a moment and then launched at Jeb. They rolled around on the ground for a while until exhaustion set in.

"What are the humans doing?" asked a Boer.

"I've seen our humans do that with the little one," bleated Rocky. "I think they're playing."

"Hee-hee-hee-hee . . . you dumbass losers, rollin' around in our shit," said a toothless man. Just then, his plastic bucket gave way from the heat of the fire, and he went tumbling to the ground.

"Hee-hee-hee-hee . . . last man standing . . . er sitting. I win!" said a bushy-eyebrowed man.

"The humans really are having a good time," bleated Rocky. "We'll be safe here tonight," and he regurgitated his cud back into his mouth for another round of chewing and swallowing. "Good night everyone."

The exhausted knife combatants laid motionless on the ground. "Hey Jeb, count the sheep over there," said the bearded man.

"One . . . two," and then Jeb passed out. After an eventful night of drinking, the other homeless men passed out too.

*   *   *

The morning sun peeked over the horizon and the herd stirred. The homeless men did not. "Good morning," bleated Penny to Tomás at her side. She stood up and winced. "Yow! That's not good."

Tomás stood up too. "What's wrong?"

"Strangest thing, my teats hurt."

"You're probably hungry and it's just your stomach."

Another Nubian doe stood up and winced. "Argh!" she bleated.

"You too?" asked Tomás. "Your teats?"

"Yeah, most definitely."

"What's goin' on here? Why don't you ladies try eating some weeds." The does grazed for a moment and then a third doe stood up and exclaimed, "Eeeyouch! My teats!"

Soon the entire herd was on the move. The bearded homeless man sat up and rubbed his eyes. "Bye bye little goats, next time we're gonna eatcha!" and he laid back down again. The herd walked briskly, stopping occasionally to pick at the weeds, when it came to a creek. By now all five of the Nubian does were in pain and the bucks were becoming concerned.

"Everyone should drink some water," bleated Rocky. "Hopefully the ladies will feel better." The herd inched down the grassy creek embankment and sucked on refreshing snowmelt water that flowed over a bed of silty sand and cobble, through a thicket of tule reeds on its sinuous journey to the Rex River.

"You make loud drinking noises like the little one back home," bleated Gordie to a ewe.

"I say ol' boy," replied the ewe, "you're not exactly quiet yourself."

"I suppose we're all a bit loud," added Tomás, "because we're thirsty. Drink up everyone." After everyone had their fill, the herd emerged from the creek refreshed and with clean hooves. "Don't you feel a whole lot better?" asked Tomás. "Ready to keep walking?"

The herd milled about without answering, and Rocky posed another question. "Ladies, how are the teats?" The

Nubian does all shook their heads. "Oh, not the answer we wanted. Tomás, what should we do about the ladies?"

Tomás thought for a moment. "I don't think we can do anything. Maybe with time they'll get better. What we can do is keep walking to a pasture without mean dogs, to a place we can call home."

"You're pushing us awfully hard. Can't we just graze here for a while?"

Tomás looked around. "Graze on the usual weeds?" He put his nose in the air. "I smell something much better. Something I can't quite identify. I think we should keep going. It'll be all right, you'll see."

The herd reluctantly moved on, following the creek should more drinking be necessary. In the distance a strange metal tube rose from the creek to an equally strange bell-shaped object on the creek bank, and a faint hum filled the air. "What's that?" asked a Boer, but no one could answer.

When they got closer the hum became a growl, and Rocky had an answer. "Be careful, it's another making of the humans." The herd carefully skirted around the irrigation pump into a lush green pasture, avoiding the spray of several impulse sprinklers.

Penny wagged her tail. "You may have found our place, Tomás. The water sprays just like at home."

They walked further, into a field of strawberries. "This is the smell!" shouted Tomás. "It's like nothing I've ever smelled before. Isn't it wonderful? Let us feast!" The herd dispersed throughout the strawberry field, plucking the sweet red berries as rhythmically as Jimi Hendrix would pluck his electric guitar. It was music to their bellies.

"I have to say, you've led us well," bleated a Boer to Tomás.

"Thanks. Did you get enough to eat?"

"I'm still workin' on it, and later I'll certainly enjoy second meal. Third meal will—"

A shot rang out and the Boer dropped to the ground. The herd instinctively scattered, but Tomás came back to check on his fallen comrade. "Hey there, won't you get up?" The Boer was bleeding and still, dead from a pinpoint bullet strike to the head. He nudged the Boer with his nose. "We really must be going now, come—" A second shot whizzed by Tomás' head, and he ran to join the others.

They had assembled by the creek just downstream of the irrigation pump, nervously prancing about with fear of the inexplicable. "What happened Tomás?" asked Penny.

"I don't know. Our friend leaks the red of those who don't wake up. We need to get outta here."

"But that's Bernie back there," objected Rocky, "you can't just leave him there."

"We must, it's too danger—" A third shot ricocheted off the irrigation pump, the loud ding drowning out the growl of the pump motor and scaring the herd further downstream.

They ran for several minutes, and regrouped under some "snowing" cottonwood trees on the creek bank. Rocky was agitated. "I'm not happy with you Tomás. Bernie was one of my kind, and now he doesn't wake because of you."

"I'm sorry about Bernie. I just wanted us to have some treats, something besides the usual weeds, to help get us through this hard journey to a new home."

"It's not just Bernie, it's also the two others who don't wake because you led us to the animals with white eyes and red eyes."

"Oh relax Rocky," bleated Gordie as he rolled onto his back pointing his legs straight up into the air as if he'd fainted. "Relax like—"

"That's an old act Gordie, and it's not funny."

"I'm just saying don't blame Tomás for everything. After all, he did lead us away from the mean dogs back home, and I'm sure he'll lead us to a great new home."

"Lead us away, did he? He couldn't even nose the shiny stick on top of the white wood to let us walk through. I had to do that. He pushes us too hard on this journey, not letting us stop to graze and rest nearly enough. And our ladies are sick thanks to him."

"That's not fair!" cried Penny.

"What's not fair is the abuse we're taking on this journey. I've had enough." He looked at his fellow Boers. "Come on guys, let's go back home."

"You'll never make it," bleated Tomás. "And even if you do, the mean dogs are waiting there for you."

"Are you gonna stop me?" Rocky reared up on his hind legs, and then Tomás did the same.

"Stop it!" yelled Penny. "You're friends." They cocked their heads, paused for a second to stare down each other, and then Tomás dropped his front legs to the ground.

"Not anymore," he bleated. "You can go."

"We want to follow you," bleated a ewe to Rocky, "to avoid the sickness the other ladies have," and she and the other ewe lined up behind Rocky.

"Very well," bleated Rocky, and he led the two other Boers and the two ewes away without as much as a look over his shoulder at the Nubians he once knew.

*　　*　　*

The herd numbered only seven now— Tomás, Gordie, Penny, and the four other Nubian does. They watched as Rocky and the others faded away on their trek upstream along the creek beneath a cloudless afternoon sky.

"Well, that's it," bleated Gordie, "they're really gone."

"Gone and forgotten," added Tomás. He surveyed the faces next to him and saw a tired and hungry bunch. "Maybe Rocky was right about one thing though, me pushing too hard. Would everyone like stay here and eat for a while?" The group nodded in agreement. "Okay then, we eat while they walk."

The menu consisted of a star thistle appetizer, a knapweed main course, and a mustard plant dessert. On tap was cool refreshing water in the adjacent creek. After it consumed the last of the spines, flowers, stems, leaves, and seeds, the herd laid down to ruminate . . . and to dream.

"After third meal we'll follow the water to a better place," proclaimed Tomás.

"Do you really think so?" asked a doe.

"I know so."

"To a place with blackberries?"

"And with the sweet red berries."

"Will the humans stroke our heads?"

"And stroke the hollow wood and howl like a dog."

An annoying buzz suddenly interrupted their conversation. "What's that noise?" asked the doe.

"It's a hummingbird," bleated Penny.

"That's no hummingbird," added Tomás, "it's too big, and it has four legs and four wings."

"Another making of the humans?" pondered Gordie.

The herd got up and cautiously followed the buzz to a knoll on which a tree like no other it had ever seen rose high into the air. The tree had uniform branches that grew sparsely from a brown trunk that was almost shiny.

"Now what's it doing?" asked a doe. "It's so close to the tree."

"Maybe it has a nest there," bleated Penny. "What a bad place for a nest, the tree looks so sick."

Suddenly Gordie pranced around atop the knoll "Over there!" he yelled. "Look below . . . across the wide water. Do you see them?"

Tomás strained to see. "I do! I see humans sitting down, and many others like us eating the weeds."

The drone completed its cell tower inspection and flew away, and the herd excitedly climbed down the knoll to be with the other goats at a better place— on the waterside slope of the Rex River levee. But first it had more to climb down. A lot more. It had a 50-foot rocky bluff to climb down.

Tomás and Gordie slowly led the ladies down the bluff, crisscrossing the bluff face in search of tiny ledges to place their agile hooves for maneuvering. "This kind of walking comes naturally," bleated Tomás, "how's everyone doing?"

"Doin' alright," replied Gordie, and he looked above. "Ladies?"

"We're okay," answered Penny. "This would be a whole lot easier without our teats feeling like—" And that's when one of her back hooves slipped, sending rock fragments below. "Watch out!" she yelled, and she dug in hard with her front hooves.

Instinctively Tomás looked up, and took a blow to the head. The cut from a jagged chunk of rock was the least of his worries; his main concern was how to navigate the remaining 20 feet of bluff after losing his purchase on the bluff face. He scrambled wildly along the rocks as long as he could, sending his own shower of rock fragments below, but ultimately had to leap the last 10 feet. The impact was forceful and shot a column of water skyward, for Tomás had bellyflopped into a deep pool of water below the cascading creek that they had followed.

"Tomás! Are you alright?" shouted Penny.

"I think so," he replied while quickly paddling ashore. Moments later the herd joined him.

"Oh . . . your cheek is bleeding," bleated Penny, "and it's all my fault." She walked over to nuzzle him. "I'm sorry."

"It's nothing."

"With the ladies sick and now Tomás leaking red, looks like I'm the only healthy one around here," bleated Gordie, " and some would say my head's not right."

"Aren't we quite the group," observed a doe.

"And now you're gonna have to get wet like me," bleated Tomás. "We're gonna cross the wide water right here to join the others. Just look at them, eating weeds with humans close by. Why I bet those humans feed them grain at night like ours did."

The herd walked along the creek below the deep pool of water which had saved Tomás from further injury, or worse, and entered the Rex River at the confluence. The Rex was slow and shallow near the shore, and the herd walked slowly ahead with hooves planting precariously on the slippery cobble riverbed.

It inched further and deeper into the Rex, the cold snowmelt water taking everyone's breath away and zapping them of energy. "Easy does it everyone," bleated Tomás. "If our feet stop touching the bottom you'll have to kick like you've never kicked before."

"My feet barely touch," bleated a doe.

"Mine too," bleated another.

"Okay, this is it everyone. Kick! . . . Kick! . . . Kick!" shouted Tomás.

The current was much stronger as they approached the middle of the Rex, and they began to scatter like the bullet spray pattern of a lousy shooter. Each of the goats deflected along a different path— the stronger ones went fairly straight while the weaker ones bent severely downstream.

"Keep kicking everyone!" yelled Tomás, his voice aimed downstream towards those who were struggling. They approached the far shore and everyone was tired. Then came the proclamation everyone was waiting for, "I can touch!" yelled Tomás.

"Me too!" yelled Gordie.

"I can touch!" yelled a doe. Six bleats of relief called out. The seventh one didn't.

Did I hear Penny? wondered Tomás as he trudged onward over the slippery cobbles towards a well-deserved break on the far shore. Soon he and the others reached shore and began to reassemble far downstream of their target— the other goats foraging on weeds.

"Is everybody here?" asked Tomás, and the goats all looked at each other.

"Penny? Where's Penny?" asked a doe.

Tomás looked around without seeing her and became quite agitated. And then a still lump of tan and white caught his eye in the distance. "Penny!" he yelled, and he took off running. He came up to Penny, who was splayed out on the river's edge. "Penny! Penny! Are you alright?" An answer didn't come . . . and then she coughed. Tomás nosed her face and repeated, "Are you alright?"

"I've been better," she replied feebly. "Just catchin' my breath."

Tomás sighed. "Take your time. When you're ready we'll go back to the others."

She laid there a moment and then stood up. "I'm ready."

"Good, glad you're feeling better. You had me quite worried. Say, you don't want to have a go at it, do you?"

"Tomás!"

The herd was together again and, though wet and chilled to the bone, everyone had their breath and was ready to meet the other goats. They walked upstream until they couldn't walk anymore, blocked by a type of fencing that they'd never seen before— net-wire electric fencing. They easily flanked it by dipping into the shallows of the Rex, and were promptly greeted by a yapping border collie.

"Who are you?" barked Domino, the Jackson brothers' loyal watchdog.

The herd made a run for it, just as it had done to escape the coyotes back at Rodriguez Ranch only yesterday. The intruders zig-zagged through the other goats with Domino barking and nipping at their heels, but couldn't shake the badass canine.

"What the hell?" said Otis Jackson, launching up from his folding chair and squinting to see all the commotion. Maynard and Cooper followed suit, and the trio zig-zagged themselves through the goats, until Otis found Domino and issued the magic command, "Domino stop!"

The command was indeed magic and stopped everyone in their tracks. A faint cloud of dust billowed above the massive standoff, and all eyes were on the strange herd that had just infiltrated the Jacksons' levee maintenance work site. Domino, the Jackson brothers, and the 60 goats working the levee focused squarely on the intruders, who were too petrified to do anything but stare back.

During the stare down, the intruders began to speculate. "Don't move or the mean dog will attack," bleated Tomás.

"I don't think so," bleated Penny. "It seems that the human can make the mean dog nice."

"She's right," bleated the Spanish goat Number 21. "The dog isn't so mean. In fact, he's rather weak and will do whatever the human says. Just remember to eat whenever he comes around, and if you're not hungry just fake it by—"

"Enough of the stupid goat chatter!" said Otis. The wheels in his head were turning. "We seem to have some volunteer workers."

"That or some goat stew," joked Cooper.

"Looks like they're Nubians. Those are dairy goats. Can we really use some dairy goats?" asked Maynard.

"Of course we can," replied Otis. They eat, don't they? We just won't milk 'em."

"Let's see," said Maynard pointing at the Nubians, "there's one . . . two . . . three . . . four . . . five does. And by the looks of it their udders are about to burst. They gotta be hurtin'.'"

"And two bucks besides the does," added Cooper, "and none of 'em with any horns. Our goats will have their way with 'em."

"Maybe," said Otis, "but we can't turn down seven free workers. We'll get this damn job done faster for the bureaucrats. Let 'em eat the weeds and get accustomed to our herd. Keep Domino away so they feel more at ease. Then we'll load 'em up in the trailers when we leave tonight. It'll be cozy in there but nothing that the goats can't handle."

The Jacksons' three goat trailers were quite full on the monotonous ride home, but the gas tanks in their three pickup trucks weren't. They stopped at the Zivkovic Mini-Mart and got gas, both the intended and unintended varieties, for the cups of chili sold there were renowned regionally. Made from an old family recipe, the chili included tender angus beef, lots of chile, and brown ale, and was prepared by Grandma Zivkovic herself.

The brothers ate in the cabs of their pickups while the gas pump meters spun wildly. They occupied three of the four filling bays and drew curious stares from the occupants of the car in the fourth bay. For the goats the refueling was a respite from bouncing around in the moving trailers, and they could relax and have a conversation.

"Bienvenidos amigos . . . welcome friends," bleated the Spanish goat Number 44.

"Thanks," acknowledged Penny.

"I like your ears," added Gordie, "they're so . . . interesting."

"Yeah, I get that a lot."

"Where are you from?" asked a Savanna, Number 51.

"We come from a place," replied Tomás, "where birds can splash in water and we can stand on rocks, where water sprays the pasture and our ladies squirt white, where the humans are good and give us first meal."

"Our humans give us dry grass sometimes," bleated Number 51, "but usually we ride the shaking shed to a place where we eat weeds."

"Tell 'em about your brother," bleated another Savanna. Number 51 shook his head and buried it between two other goats. "Go on, tell 'em."

Number 51 regained his composure. "Okay, I will. My brother was trying to eat some blackberries and got his head tangled in shiny ropes that bit him. A human finally got him out of the ropes, but after that he didn't feel well."

"Maybe eating weeds or drinking water did him some good?" surmised Tomás.

"It didn't. In fact, he felt worse, and that night a human came to check on him. That's when we heard a terrible cry and saw the human leave holding something sharp and flat and shiny covered in red. I never saw my brother again."

"Are you saying the human made your brother leak red and not wake up?"

"What do you think?" Tomás suddenly felt a pain in his gut worse than that of the does, and he and the other goats began to bounce around again as the pickups drove away.

*   *   *

The abducted goats didn't sleep well at Jackson Goat Ranch that night. The engorged udders of the does were even more painful now, and they shifted around in the dilapidated goat barn all night in search of a comfortable position on the dirt floor laden with droppings. Tomás and Gordie didn't fare much better with a lot on their minds. "I'm starting to wonder about this place Tomás," bleated Gordie.

"Me too. Many of the others have big horns and look mean."

"And we know the dog can be mean, unless the humans make him nice."

"Right, but I think our biggest concern, the thing that makes me want to escape, is that we've been told even the humans can be mean."

"You want to escape?"

Tomás nodded. "In the morning we'll look for a shiny stick on top of white wood. That's our way out."

At the crack of dawn, Tomás and Gordie walked the extensive fence line atJackson Goat Ranch and their hope of escape all but vanished. "Where's the white wood with a shiny stick on top?" observed Tomás. "There's only the shiny ropes we were told about. I wonder if they really do bite. Go ahead, touch 'em Gordie."

"Me? No way! You touch 'em."

"Hey, what are you new guys doin'?" shouted Number 35, a large Boer approaching them from behind.

Tomás and Gordie jumped. "Nothin'," bleated Gordie. "Just lookin' around."

"Lookin' around, huh? You're not getting out. We've tried before, and every time the shiny ropes bite us."

"But the humans must go through the ropes," bleated Tomás, "we just need to find out where."

"Oh, we know where. They go where the top of the ropes is black. The ropes bite us but not them."

"That's odd."

"Sure is. Let me know if you figure it out, I'll go through the ropes with you."

"Okay," and Tomás and Gordie trotted away. They found the black plastic handle of the gate in the net-wire electric fencing and pondered, but their minds quickly turned to other matters— two more large Boers approached them, Number 18 and Number 19.

"Hey new guys, that's our spot!" yelled Number 18.

Tomás was dumbfounded. "Huh?"

"That's our spot. We like to stand there."

"We were only trying to—"

"I don't need to listen to you, you're a runt without horns. And from the look of that nasty cut on your cheek you're probably a troublemaker."

"Listen, we're not looking for any—"

"I don't like you. Why don't you move away."

Tomás and Gordie walked along the fence for a minute. The Boers followed. "That's our spot too," bleated Number 19.

"Look, we're in a huge field," bleated Tomás, "there's plenty of spots for all of us."

Without warning, the Boers rammed their long twisted horns into the ribs of Tomás and Gordie. The pain was intense, but when they stumbled and became entangled in the net-wire electric fencing, the pain became excruciating.

"That's a good spot for you," bleated Number 19, and he and Number 18 walked away.

Tomás and Gordie thrashed about in the electrified fencing and, without having any horns to get caught in the small openings of the netting, getting untangled was relatively easy. "You okay?" asked Tomás after they were free.

"Aside from my ribs hurting and my whole body tingling, I'm just great. And you?"

"I'm okay. That was bad. Never again do I want to feel the bite of the shiny ropes. Can you believe those guys? If only we had horns." They lumbered back to the barn and were promptly greeted with yet another assault.

"Get in here!" yelled Otis, and he and Cooper pushed Tomás and Gordie into the barn and slammed shut the door. Most of the other goats were inside and watching, including the Nubian does who seemed agitated and paced around.

"Watch out!" yelled Penny. "They're gonna poke you." She turned her head and showed Tomás a bright blue tag on her ear. Inscribed was the number 61.

It was too late. Cooper had Tomás in a headlock and Otis centered a bright blue tag on his ear. Otis squeezed the handles of the tagger and a pin pierced Tomás' ear and secured the tag. "Ahhhhh!" screamed Tomás, and he jerked away from Cooper and ran through the barn. Gordie was next and screamed even louder. When it was over Tomás and Gordie were no more, they were Number 66 and Number 67.

"Alright, that's that," said Otis, "let's get 'em loaded up." The brothers backed up their pickup trucks with attached trailers to the gate in the electric fencing, and the goats began their morning pilgrimage up ramps leading to the trailers.

"Keep goin' dumbasses!" yelled Maynard, tapping the goats' butts with a crook to hurry along the procession up the ramp to the trailer that he was towing.

"For you, mi amigo," bleated Number 21 at the top of the ramp, and he expelled some droppings.

"Interesting time for that," observed Gordie.

"It was a message for the human who shakes our shed."

"Nice!" and Gordie left his own pile of droppings at the top of the ramp.

The goats were silent on the ride to the levee maintenance work site. They bounced around in the trailers, anticipating another day of drudgery and contrived meals of weeds, which proliferated on the Rex River levee.

PART 4 — THE PINEAPPLE EXPRESS

"When a storm blows, you must stand firm. For it is not trying to knock you down, it is really trying to teach you to be strong."
—*Joseph M. Marshall III, Native American Writer/Historian*

7

A STORM BREWS

A pril 2

Hank Hartman of KCLM NewsChannel 7 knew his stuff. He had to, because he sure didn't have the striking looks of a typical television weatherman. He was 63 and balding and wore a gray suit one size too small. He had a microphone clipped onto his paisley tie, a ruffled kerchief in the breast pocket of his blazer, and a nerdy lightning bolt pin on his lapel. His thin circular wire-rimmed eyeglasses looked like Hitler's, but his mustache certainly didn't, a long bushy growth approaching caterpillar status.

The locals in the Rex River Valley just loved Hank and depended on him to deliver an accurate forecast. He usually did— whether it called for a hot spell, a cold snap, a windy day, or a wet storm, the locals got the information they needed to go about their daily lives. Farmers could anticipate their irrigation needs, parents would know when to bundle their children in heavy jackets for school, city and county maintenance workers could prepare for downed branches, and shoppers would know when to tote their umbrellas to the malls.

Hank had a lot to say about today's weather and the forecast, and he spoke quickly in his four minutes of air time. He clicked the remote in his hand to switch from map to map, showing such weather features as the highs and lows, the fronts and temperatures, and the isobars and wind vectors. Then he clicked to the most recent satellite image and practically salivated; a big storm was much more interesting than a string of 75-degree days. He was truly excited about the forecast, and it showed in his delivery. His arms gyrated enthusiastically at the satellite image behind him, a little too enthusiastically, and below his tight blazer he exposed a worn belt and a pudgy belly when he pointed too high.

"Just look at this picture folks, a long narrow band of moisture extending all the way from south of Hawaii to California. And we expect a strong jet stream aloft to bring all that warm moist air right here to the Rex River Valley and to the mountains above Ol' Hemhuck. Your local creeks will fill and the major rivers like the Rex and the Orion will run high and swift. All you bikers and hikers out there, expect the trails along those rivers to be submerged for days to come."

"The first rain should arrive tomorrow morning around nine, and it won't let up for most of the week. The rain totals will be massive, especially in the mountains where we don't expect much snow out of this warm storm. We'll be keeping an eye on the inflows to Ol' Hemhuck, and on the stream levels throughout the area in the next several days, so keep it right here at NewsChannel 7. Back to you Roger."

8

THE RAIN FALLS

April 3-April 7

Hank Hartman was right. Heavy dark clouds did drift in around nine in the morning, and a raindrop formed. It fell diagonally to earth at terminal velocity, deflected by the strong winds aloft and taking on the aerodynamic shape of a teardrop. It was a warm drop of 70 degrees Fahrenheit, and it was a special drop— the first of an uncountable number of raindrops that would fall over the Rex River Watershed in the next five days.

Meteorologists call a long narrow band of moisture in the atmosphere, which Hank so enthusiastically identified, an atmospheric river. Moisture from the tropics flows like a river in the sky, and it's released as large amounts of rain or snow when it makes landfall. When the river in the sky originates near Hawaii and extends all the way to the west coast of the United States, it's called a Pineapple Express. That's exactly what charged towards residents of the Rex

River Watershed, a Pineapple Express, without any Aloha spirit.

The warm deluge of the Pineapple Express infiltrated and melted the ripe snowpack in the upper elevations of the Rex River Watershed. The resulting rainwater and snowmelt runoff gushed downhill, over saturated loams and impermeable granite outcroppings to join the rainwater runoff from the lower elevations. The growing flood of water became more defined in brooks and creeks and ultimately formed a dendritic network of tributaries that discharged into the swelling Rex.

The inflows to Ol' Hemhuck rose abruptly for two days, and peaked on the third day after the most intense rain had fallen. The lake level rose rapidly, despite all three outlet gates being wide open, until the ungated concrete spillway started to flow.

The spillway discharged excess water down a steep concrete chute which flipped upward at the end and dramatically sprayed the water through the air into a stilling basin that drained into the Rex, dissipating the immense hydraulic energy of the rushing water. Despite the spillway spewing water and the inflows receding on the fourth day, the lake level still rose slowly, and Hank Hartman was there to cover it.

Hank's face was saturated and he spat rainwater onto his microphone when he spoke. "You can see the beautiful spray of water just behind me," he said of the spillway discharge, "like water being shot from fireboat hoses on the Fourth of July." The nearly horizontal rain pummeled him and he stumbled a step. His hooded blue KCLM raincoat glistened with rainwater. "What you can't see is the lake level, which I'm told will crest and then recede tomorrow morning as lake inflows continue to decrease." Hank wiped the rainwater off of his wire-rimmed eyeglasses. *That's better*, he thought, *I can see again, but I still can't feel my toes.* "Back to you Roger."

9

A WARNING DISMISSED

April 8

Megan Riley, the young engineering prodigy at Ol' Hemhuck Water District came barging into the office of Robert Sutton, President of the district's Board of Directors. She was breathless, and her hooded yellow rubber raincoat and black rubber boots dripped water freely. She lowered her hood and spoke between gasps of air. "I was just at Ol' Hemhuck . . . the seepage by the outlets has increased . . . and the water color is brown . . . soil is being carried away . . . the dam's going to fail . . . and we need to blow the alarm whistle."

"Now, now young lady," said Robert, "take a deep breath and relax. I think you're overreacting. We wouldn't want to panic our fine valley residents going about their daily busi-ness by blowing the alarm whistle, would we? Ol' Hemhuck isn't going anywhere. She's been around since before your grandparents were born and has withstood the test of time. And now with this severe storm she's passed unprecedented spillway flows without any problems. Sure, the lake elevation hit at an all-time high this morning, but it's well below the top of the dam and it's falling."

"With all due respect, sir, you need to get your head out of the sand!"

"Alright young lady, that's enough!"

"I know what I saw. It was real, and it will lead to dam failure. The science says so."

Robert sighed. "Alright, tell you what I'll do. The storm's almost over. Tomorrow's supposed to be a sunny day. I'll put together a team to come take a look tomorrow."

"That'll be too late."

"Don't be so sure young lady. This engineering marvel you're so worried about, Ol' Hemhuck, it's indestructible."

"But sir—"

"Tomorrow! We'll look at it tomorrow!"

Pointless, thought Megan, and she ran out of Robert's office, leaving behind a large puddle of water where she had stood and a desperate plea that Robert would never heed. She pulled out her phone in the adjoining hallway and called her friend and neighbor. "Trish, this is Megan, listen to me carefully."

Trish sensed the urgency in Megan's voice. "What's wrong?"

"Ol' Hemhuck is going to fail. Maybe today, maybe tomorrow, but soon. You need to get out of your house now."

"Seriously? But I thought it couldn't—"

"It can, and it will. And tell a neighbor, and have them tell another. We've got to clear the neighborhood."

PART 5 — THE VALLEY REELS

"All the world is full of suffering. It is also full of over-coming."
—*Hellen Keller, American Author/Disability Rights Activist*

10

A SUNNY DAY

April 9, 8:05 a.m.

The goats were silent and bounced around in the trailers once again on the ride to the Rex River levee maintenance work site. It had been a week since their last ride since the Jacksons didn't take them to work during the stormy weather, an undertaking that would have been miserable for all. But the day was beautiful and sunny and the Jacksons were eager to finish this last reach of work before collecting a big paycheck. It spanned between the Yellow Chick Lane Bridge and the mighty Orion River, on the west side of the Rex— the east side had no levee, just the bluff from which Tomás had fallen.

The brothers parked on the levee crest and set up the net-wire electric fencing to prevent goats on the landside slope from wandering too far and wreaking havoc on the fertile farmland dotted with houses and barns. They knew the Rex River, flowing high and swift, brown with silt, and full of floating logs and vegetal debris, would undoubtedly prevent goats on the waterside slope from straying that way.

The goats filed out of the trailers and down the ramps. Domino was there to greet any loiterers on the levee crest. "Start eating," he barked threateningly, "or I'll eat you," his bark being bigger than his bite. He nipped at their heels and they scattered throughout the work site.

"Hurry along now," said Maynard to Number 21, his Spanish goat nemesis. The goat pulled a heavy wooden cart loaded with full ice chests, an empty tub, gallons of drinking water for the goats, folding chairs, and as punishment some rocks. The leather harness cut tightly across Number 21's chest, and he was breathing hard by the time Maynard stopped him at a prime viewing spot on the levee crest in the middle of the work site. "Back from whence ye came," shouted Maynard, and he threw the rocks back onto the levee and unloaded the cart.

He poured the drinking water into the tub, then sat in a folding chair and popped open his morning beer. Otis and Cooper joined him for beer after pouring more drinking water, which Number 21 had carried for them in the cart, into their tubs at each end of the work site. "Ever see the river so high?" asked Otis.

"Uh-uh," replied the twins together.

"Ever see such a happy dog? That Domino just loves harassing the goats."

Cooper squinted. "Are those the new goats he's harassing?"

Maynard squinted too. "Yup, think so. What a good boy!"

The brothers kicked back in their chairs and drained the first of many beers while the goats worked on the levee. They walked on the landside and waterside slopes, not unlike a pirate walks the plank or a drunk walks the line. Forced by beings in control, they ate thick pockets of star thistle, poison oak, mustard plant, pepperweed, and other invasives, and treaded lightly on the saturated levee slopes, leaving shallow hoof prints in the ground.

Tomás, Gordie, and the does started picking at a patch of mustard plant. Satisfied at their efforts, Domino trotted away. "I thought he'd never shut up," bleated Gordie. "One day I swear I'm gonna butt that dog."

"You and the rest of us," added Tomás.

The does were feeling much better. Their milk had dried up during the week of the Pineapple Express, and they could move again without feeling like their teats were on fire.

"Hey girls," bleated Number 18, one of the large Boers who had annihilated Tomás and Gordie. "Stay still so we can have our way with you."

"Yeah, stay still," echoed Number 19, the other large Boer annihilator.

The does looked up, their teeth dangling the yellow of mustard plant. "What's your problem?" bleated Penny.

The Boers moved in behind the does, and raised their front legs onto the backs of two of them. The does tried to run away, but the strength of the Boers kept them there. "Get off!" they yelled.

"Help them!" yelled Penny, and Tomás and Gordie charged in. Without hesitation they rammed the Boers, whose attention was definitely elsewhere, and dislodged them from their mounts. The two does ran away and the Boers confronted their assailants.

"Look who's here," bleated Number 18, "the new guys."

"Remember us?" added Number 19. "We showed you the right spot in our field."

Tomás had a sinking feeling, but he put up a brave front. "It was a bad spot, where the shiny ropes bit us."

"You thought that was bad? When we're through with you you'll be under the wide water forever." Number 18 and Number 19 flashed their long twisted horns at Tomás and Gordie, then reared up on their hind legs to strike. Instinctively Tomás and Gordie reared up too, hornless and outweighed by the large Boers.

Just then, Spanish goats Number 21 and Number 44 appeared, having heard the commotion. "Alto!" yelled Number 21. No one understood, but his emphatic tone got everyone to drop their front legs to the ground and look at him. "Now then, what's going on here?"

"I know," bleated Number 44, looking disgustedly at the Boers. "These two are always mean to me and mis amigas. I always tell mis amigas not to mate them. I saw them looking for mates and then they forced themselves on the new girls."

"Is that true?" asked Number 21. "Did you force yourselves on the new girls?"

"So what if we did," bleated Number 18.

"Yeah, so what if we did," echoed Number 19.

The fury was building up in Number 21. "That's not how to treat new friends. Don't you understand?"

The Boers looked at each other. "We understand the strong get their way," bleated Number 18. "We're strong, so you need to get out of our way."

The fury in Number 21 boiled over and he charged Number 18 who was ready and waiting. They rammed horns and a great crack rattled the air. Number 19 arrived a split second later, ramming his powerful horns into the ribs of Number 21. Tomás and Gordie joined in the fray, ramming Number 19 the best they could with their hornless heads. It was a scrum with no rugby ball, a fight with no end, until Domino arrived on scene with mouth blazing. "That's enough . . . break it up . . . go eat . . . go eat now!" he barked.

Maynard heard the ruckus, jumped to his feet, and ran to the chaos. He didn't get there as a gopher hole had other plans for him— a bellyflop, an impressive 10-foot slide down the muddy waterside levee slope, a mouthful of mud, plugged nostrils, blurred vision, and most tragically a massive rip in the crotch of his new pair of jeans. "Goddamn gopher hole!" he shouted.

The scrum had dispersed, except for Number 21 who, like Maynard, slowly picked himself off of the ground. Otis and Cooper laughed hysterically at their brother and gave him a standing ovation. "Nice work Maynard!" shouted Otis. "We'll be sure to mark that gopher hole for the bureaucrats to fill." They clapped some more and whistled loudly by blowing through their fingers.

Then a real whistle blew. It was the noon whistle, only it wasn't noon. Otis recovered enough from the hilarity to dig out his phone from his pants pocket. "Nine thirty-eight," he read. "Some whistle blower don't know how to tell time."

11

MONOLITH NO MORE

April 9, 9:10 a.m.

Ol' Hemhuck dwarfed the four people standing below it. They wore clear plastic ponchos and white hardhats imprinted with the Ol' Hemhuck Water District logo— a blue drop of water overlaying a large flowering almond tree. It was District Board President Robert Sutton's inspection team, thrown together rather hastily to appease the vocal and bothersome engineer Megan Riley, who carried a tablet for taking pictures. The other team members included geotechnical and hydraulic specialists and Robert Sutton himself.

They stood at the base of the rock-faced embankment, facing the three wide open outlet gates and the steep concrete spillway chute which flipped upward at the end. They struggled to hear each other over the noise of the rushing water, and to see through the spray of the spillway. They were wet from the spray, but Megan periodically raised her tablet to take pictures and then wiped it off on the shirt underneath her poncho. "Look at this," she shouted, and the others leaned in to her tablet. "Here, let me enlarge it." She touched the tablet screen and spread her fingers. "Can you see it?"

They stared a moment at the enlarged image, and then the hydraulic specialist shouted, "Brown water, seeping under the dam to the right of the outlet gates."

"I don't like it," shouted the geotechnical specialist.

"But some seepage is normal," shouted Robert, maintaining his rosy position even though his stomach now began to churn.

Since the construction of Ol' Hemhuck in the 1930s, hydrostatic forces have pressed on the defective soil compaction around its three outlet conduits. The greatest hydrostatic forces were during periods of high lake levels, and no lake level was higher than yesterday during the Pineapple Express. The torrential rainstorm was a gut punch, a kick to the groin, a body slam, and Ol' Hemhuck felt it.

Deep within Ol' Hemhuck, the soil compacted around its three outlet conduits was on the move. And then, it happened. A small sinkhole appeared on the downstream face of the dam, to the right of the outlet gates about 10 feet up. The sinkhole allowed water to seep through the dam, and the sinkhole size grew exponentially. Nothing could stop this runaway train now, and a catastrophic breach was imminent.

"Oh my God!" shouted Megan after spotting the sinkhole in her next enlarged picture.

"What is it?" asked Robert, eyes wide open with concern.

"It's happening! The dam's starting to fail! We gotta get outta here, and we gotta sound the alarm whistle!" They ran for their lives with ponchos flapping in the breeze, along the base of the rock-faced embankment to a metal stairway. Everyone sprinted up the stairway without stopping to rest at any of the four landings, except Robert. At 81 years old and with a trick knee, Robert was hunched over and gasping for air on the third landing.

The stairway ended on top of the eastside bluff which overlooked Ol' Hemhuck and the Rex, and joined a sidewalk that led to the Ol' Hemhuck Water District field office building. "You're safe there," yelled Megan to Robert from the top, gasping for air herself. "I'll come back for you . . . but first I need permission . . . to blow the alarm whistle." Robert remained hunched over and didn't respond. "President Sutton . . . I need permission to blow the alarm whistle," she yelled louder.

Fueled by the oxygen in more breaths, Robert regained some strength and looked up at Megan and slowly nodded. She took off like a cheetah before the last nod, sprinted down the sidewalk, and barged into the field office building. A man at a desk stopped tapping his keyboard to see what was going on. "Hi Megan," he said. "Can I help you?"

"Where's the alarm button?" she demanded.

"But it's not noon, it's only nine—"

"I know what time it is! The dam's failing, I need to push the damn button!"

The man sized her up— the pooling water below her drenched poncho, the tablet she tapped nervously, the heavy breathing, the absolute terror on her face. "Right there," he said, and pointed by the water cooler. Megan was there in a flash, shot her index finger forward, and pressed firmly on the alarm button. She let out a huge sigh of relief and stared at the half full water cooler for a moment. *Not much water in there,* she thought. *If only Ol' Hemhuck had that much.* Tears welled up in her eyes. It was 9:38 a.m.

The alarm whistle started as a low drone and built up to a high-pitched whine before dropping down to the low drone again. It sounded from a nearby hilltop, stopping residents of the Rex River Valley in their tracks— customers shopping in stores, children studying at school, farmers tending their fields, seniors walking their dogs. Some of them checked their watches, others looked skyward or all around, but those familiar with the area and the emergency protocol headed for higher ground.

Ol' Hemhuck, that indestructible dam, was crumbling. That first small sinkhole about 10 feet up had grown to a massive breach extending halfway up the downstream face of the dam. A raging river of brown poured from the breach into the already swollen Rex, which filled to the brink of spilling onto the low-lying farmlands to the west. And Hank Hartman was there to cover it all for KCLM NewsChannel 7.

Normally a fast talker, Hank spoke even faster into his microphone as the events behind him unfolded rapidly. "Behind me you can see a huge hole in Ol' Hemhuck, with tons of rock and dirt being carried away. This is serious folks. If you live on the west side and you're watching me— don't! Get out! Leave your home and seek higher ground."

He turned to his cameraman. "Joe, if you can pan in front of me our viewers can see the Horsefly Road Bridge." Four cars passed over the steel truss bridge with three spans, a busy two-lane arterial. "Just look at all the logs and debris piling up on the bridge piers . . . and some of it's even hitting the bottom of the bridge."

Brown frothy water battered the logs and debris against the bridge, and water started spilling over the bridge deck. Suddenly the center span gave way. "Oh . . . Oh no!" yelled Hank. "The bridge is collapsing!" Three of the cars were near the ends of the bridge and escaped disaster but the fourth car, a red Prius, fell into the raging waters and floated helplessly away.

Hank knew this was a critical moment in the broadcast and he must be eloquent. He had visions of the tragic Hindenburg broadcast and its epic catch phrase, "Oh the humanity!" *Don't say it,* he thought. *Think of something else . . . don't say it.* And then he blurted out, "Oh the car!" *Brilliant, just brilliant.*

Joe panned back to Ol' Hemhuck which was failing rapidly. "The hole in Ol' Hemhuck goes almost all the way to the top now," observed Hank. "The dam's about to come down! Again folks, you need to seek higher . . . Oh . . . Oh . . . there she goes!" A colossal mass of earth embankment sloughed into the Rex, leaving behind the now solitary concrete spillway at the western abutment, the mangled remains of the three outlet conduits, and remnants of the earth embankment at the eastern abutment.

Hank was ready to shine this time. "The monolith is no more!" he shouted. *Nice, that might just get me in the history books. Now, give 'em the solemn look . . . milk it . . . just a bit longer . . . and that's a wrap.* "Back to you Roger."

12

SURVIVAL OF THE LUCKY

April 9, 9:55 a.m.

The peak of the dam breach flood wave barreled downstream with destructive force. Anything in its path, inanimate or living, was no match for the immense wall of water traveling at 20 miles per hour. Some riparian animals were lucky and scurried to higher ground, while others were less fortunate and suffered an unpleasant watery death.

High above, a raven couple rode a convenient thermal and viewed the carnage below with their sharp eyesight. The highly intelligent birds followed the flood wave downstream, curious about the strange changes it was making to their habitat. They reached the Horsefly Road Bridge and circled above.

"The road's different," cawed the male. "I see water where the road should be."

"The water's different too," added the female. "Much faster and darker with wood floating on top. Now what?"

The male pondered a moment. "We can't eat the garbage on the road like we usually do. Let's go on."

The ravens flew to the west and scanned the flooded farmland. They saw horses and cows struggling to stay afloat, but not the countless rodents and small mammals that drowned in the floodwater. "Look," cawed the female, "water is where the crops should be."

"Then no meal here either," reasoned the male. Instinctively they crossed over the turbulent Rex to the east side bluff, and couldn't believe their eyes.

"Do you see that?" asked the male.

"Yeah, we've never seen that before!"

"All that matters is we see it now. Follow me."

The ravens dove down and strafed along the bluff face in search of an easy meal. The menu was quite full, as an abundance of animals had escaped the deadly floodwater and clung precariously to the bluff face. Squirrels, muskrats, mice, and raccoons held on for dear life, and the resourceful ravens were thrilled to pick off any one of them.

"A squirrel, dear?" asked the male.

"Yes please."

The strike was quick and fierce, and the squirrel squirmed and chirped frantically in the grasp of the raven, who airlifted it to the top of the bluff where his mate was waiting. The raven pair pecked and clawed repeatedly until the squirrel was dead, and then the feast began.

"Tastes like chicken," cawed the female.

"Better than any chicken I've ever had," added the male.

They ate for a few minutes and then stashed the remaining chunk of squirrel in a bush for later consumption. "Onward my dear," cawed the male, "to see more of the strange changes to our land and water."

The ravens flapped into the sky and soon came to another collapsed steel truss bridge at Silo Road. The brown torrent shot logs and debris into the remnants of the bridge, a large mass of twisted metal, made larger by twisted metal pieces from the collapsed Horsefly Road Bridge. Four mutilated cars were caught in the mass, and police cars were positioned at each end of the missing bridge span. Their lights flashed and their sirens blared along with the still-blowing alarm whistle that Megan had activated. Some people covered their ears and ran around in distress, while others were dumbfounded and just gawked at the bridge.

To the southwest the ravens saw Jackson Goat Ranch, now inundated by floodwater. Some ducks and geese quacked and honked above the submerged field where the goats had roamed, and the goats' wooden pallets for climbing floated randomly about like massive toy pool floats. The dilapidated barn was even more so, leaning badly with water up to its windows, and the Jacksons' three-bedroom ranch house didn't fare any better.

The ravens flew on. "What a sick tree," cawed the male, flying by the cell tower which Tomás and company had passed.

"Wouldn't want to raise our young there," added the female.

They came to the Yellow Chick Lane Bridge, which was another pile of twisted metal, and to a submerged basketball court where the basketball rims barely poked out of the water. A woman in a canoe paddled to her meowing cat stuck high in a tree, one of the few trees that wasn't uprooted.

Veering west the ravens passed over houses and barns that flooded up to their rooftops, with desperate people sitting on dry shingles awaiting rescue. An array of abandoned cars piled up along Homebrew Road beneath the murky floodwater, which muted their bright and shiny colors. Metal silos split open and leaked golden grain, which flowed away before any surviving livestock could partake in an impromptu feeding frenzy.

In the distance the ravens saw a dichotomy of merging colors, the chocolatey Rex and the bluish Orion. "Very strange," cawed the male, "these changes to our land and water."

"Strange indeed," began the female. She focused her sharp eyesight on the Rex between the Yellow Chick Lane Bridge and the Orion River. "What do you make of those white and brown spots floating in the water?"

"Goats perhaps?"

*   *   *

The peak of the flood wave hit the Jacksons' levee maintenance work site at precisely 10:04 a.m., a mere 26 minutes after Megan pushed the alarm button. Otis had ignored the whistle blower that "don't know how to tell time," and he remained in harm's way. *It's not noon, why do they keep blowin' the noon whistle?* he had thought. And then he knew why.

The realization of imminent danger hit him like a ton of bricks, and his stomach filled with butterflies. Otis heard a low rumble first, and then saw the leading edge of an immense wall of water traveling at 20 miles per hour. "Oh my God, run!" he shouted, before getting up to run.

The wall of water bowled over everything in its path— a streamflow gage below Yellow Chick Lane, willow and cottonwood trees growing by the levee, the Jacksons' pickup trucks and goat trailers parked on the levee crest, and Otis, who found himself under water fighting for his life. The impact of the water took his breath away, and the extreme current and powerful whirlpools pulled his body and limbs in directions they shouldn't be pulled. *I feel like one of Domino's ragdoll kills*, he thought, and he almost cracked a smile before blacking out.

Maynard and Cooper joined their older brother in the maelstrom, and so did the others— Domino, the 60 Jackson goats, and the seven new goats from Rodriguez Ranch. The lethal maelstrom didn't discriminate by species, breed, fitness, or any other characteristic, and only the lucky would survive.

One's position on the levee when the flood wave hit had a lot to do with one's luck. Many on the landside slope were swept away into the low-lying farmlands and faced hypothermia, entanglement in the Jacksons' electric fencing, impalement on barbed-wire fencing or any other sharp objects, blunt force trauma, and of course drowning.

Many on the waterside slope were funneled downstream into the Orion and faced similar hardships— hypothermia, blunt force trauma, and drowning, but also the torment of being pinned against boulders or bridge piers. Those on the crest, including the Jackson brothers, could go either way, to the low-lying farmlands or to the Orion.

Tomás, Gordie, Penny, and the other does had been eating mustard plant on the waterside slope when the flood wave hit, and hurtled downstream towards the Orion. "Tomás!" called out Penny. "Help me!" She kicked furiously to keep her head above the raging Rex, but the frigid water made the kicking increasingly more difficult. It cut into her like a sharp knife, and nothing could stop the bleeding. Penny felt herself slipping away by the time she reached the Orion and veered right.

The flood wave had attenuated significantly when it arrived at the larger Orion River, after the floodwater spilled throughout the Rex River Valley into the low-lying farmlands to the west, and over a short levee segment to the east beyond the end of the bluff. The Orion's larger channel capacity contained the attenuated flood wave entirely between its levees, but only by mere inches.

Gordie spotted Penny's head bobbing in the Orion, which was pretty miraculous considering his head was bobbing too. The water flowed fast, and he mustered up his strength to yell, "Penny? Is that you?"

"Gordie? Help!" Penny was swallowing water now, and much of her body was numb.

"I'll try to kick to you," shouted Gordie. They were only 100 feet apart, an easy walk from the A-frame shed to a wonderful blackberry bramble back at Rodriguez Ranch, but here in the tumultuous Orion 100 feet was like 100 miles.

They passed under the Homebrew and Shucker Road Bridges without incident and approached Kidney Bean Island, normally a bustling boater hangout but now a mostly submerged wasteland. "Kick to the land," cried Gordie, but deep down he knew Penny's efforts as well as his would be fruitless, and their fate was at the mercy of the unforgiving current.

Below Kidney Bean Island, the floodwater spilled over a concrete flood control weir into a complex of four sunken soccer fields on the south side of the Orion. The soccer fields doubled as a detention basin to capture the floodwater and reduce the dangerously high river levels downstream. But with so much water pouring in from the Ol' Hemhuck dam breach fiasco, even after flooding much of the Rex River Valley, the detention basin quickly filled up and river levels remained dangerously high downstream.

The Spanish goats Number 21 and Number 44 contorted in the frigid swirling waters of the Orion upstream of the flood control weir. And then suddenly they were still, pinned against one of the Gump Avenue Bridge piers. "Are you okay?" shouted Number 21.

Number 44 strained to hear over the water splashing against her. She and Number 21 were intertwined with an assortment of logs and debris that pressed against the bridge pier— oak and cottonwood trunks, willow branches, manzanita bushes, bed mattresses, lamp shades, and garbage. Lots of garbage. A cornucopia of waste that included plastic bottles, Styrofoam containers, cardboard boxes, and aluminum cans. "Sí," she shouted back, and turned her attention to the large red bump that already had formed on the jaw of Number 21. "How 'bout you?"

"I'll be fine. Must've butted a tree with the wrong part of my cabeza."

"I can't move, and I'm so cold. What do we do now?"

Number 21 tried to move but the current was too strong. "I don't know. We'll have to stay here 'til the water slows down." He took a long look at Number 44's cute wattles dangling from each ear, sure it would be his last, and shuddered from the cold.

After five more excruciating minutes, Number 21 and Number 44 were numb— numb to the pain, numb to the touch, numb to the severity of their quandary. And then suddenly they could feel again, the feeling of hope, after a large oak trunk rammed the logjam in which they resided. It was a one-in-a-million shot, like a bowler converting a 7-10 split, that pivoted the log they were pinned against and sent them floating down the turbulent Orion once again.

Tomás shot down the center of the Orion, spinning wildly and gasping for air. He came upon two familiar faces also struggling in the water, and felt almost elated at their predicament. He saw the panic and deep-rooted fear in the eyes of Number 18 and Number 19, his Boer nemeses, and no trace of their smirking, cocky, cruel selves. *The dirt is on the other hoof*, thought Tomás. *I must show strength. I must be in control. Let them plead to me.*

"Help! Get us outta here!" cried Number 18, exhausted and desperate.

Tomás steadied himself as best he could and bleated, "I can help. I know a good spot for you."

"Where is it? Hurry!"

"I'll show you. Hang on just a little longer. You won't have to worry about the cold and fast water anymore." They drifted out of control for another 10 seconds. "Okay," continued Tomás. "Look behind us. Do you see it? Your worries are about to be over."

Number 19 started, "I don't see any—"

Tomás ducked his head underwater, like he sometimes did to cool off while taking a drink from the water tub on a hot day back at Rodriguez Ranch, and he could clearly hear two skulls clang against the steel truss Bailey Avenue Bridge. He cleared the bridge and resurfaced, gasping for air again, and in doing a full pirouette he didn't see any sign of Number 18 or Number 19. *In the water forever*, thought Tomás, *that's a good spot for the both of you*, and then he focused his attention on surviving his nightmarish ride down the Orion.

The Orion was still dangerously high below the Bailey Avenue Bridge. Water lapped at its levee crests and threatened to overtop and breach the levees, which would inundate the affluent resort city of Darbington. Built around Lake April in the 1940s, the city of Darbington prospered after a championship golf course was built along the beautiful terminal lake. Golfers and recreationists flocked from miles away to enjoy Lake April, which typically was full even after irrigation diversions in the Rex River Valley, and they spent their money freely at the local establishments.

Crafty city planners and engineers had anticipated a doomsday scenario like the one playing out now, where the threat of levee failure and inundation of Darbington were very real. They collaborated on designing and constructing a levee feature that would minimize flood damage to the city. They created a low spot in the north levee of the Orion, one foot lower than the rest of the levee crest, to be the designated overtopping and breaching spot.

A levee failure there would flood the blighted Estes neighborhood and spare from flooding the expensive downstream residential and commercial properties around Lake April. The plan was overwhelmingly approved since mostly rundown properties would be damaged in the unlikely event that the Orion ever flowed too high.

Disoriented now from hypothermia, Tomás floated towards the Estes neighborhood. His thoughts jumped from good times with his true love Penny to the whereabouts of his rebellious friend Rocky, from the human stroking the hollow wood to the wonderful garden smells that wafted in back home, from riding in the shaking shed with strangers to—

What's that? he wondered. A strange structure interrupted his foggy thinking. *A barn? No, it can't be. Doesn't matter anyway. Nothing matters anymore.* His eyes closed as he floated by the abandoned Estes Catholic Church, with its shattered windows boarded up and its tall spire leaning badly and propped up by metal scaffolding.

*   *   *

By 12:10 p.m. Ol' Hemhuck reached an eerie equilibrium. The rain and snowmelt runoff came in just as fast as it went out through the dam's large trapezoidal breach, with a bottom width of 450 feet, a top width of 750 feet, and a height of 150 feet. The lake behind Ol' Hemhuck was gone, and the Rex became the unregulated river it once was.

In the aftermath of the dam breach, Ol' Hemhuck's enormous volume of impounded water now submerged a vast area of land, dealing hardships on far too many animals and people. At a flooded farm a bewildered man stared at rows upon rows of almond treetops, his cash crop almost completely inundated and his livelihood most definitely in turmoil. He sat in a row boat with his wife, who wept openly as he paddled towards their flooded house.

On Kidney Bean Island a distraught man sat on the undercarriage of his inverted red Prius, perched precariously in the branches of a cottonwood tree which bent and swayed in the swift waters. His blood-stained clothes were ripped, and he sat alone clutching a soggy teddy bear to his heart, shivering and crying uncontrollably over the little one he'd lost upstream in the Rex.

In the Estes neighborhood of Darbington a single mom read to her two daughters by candlelight in the bedroom of their second-floor apartment which had lost power in the flood. They huddled together eating popcorn and even laughed occasionally, making the best of a bad but tenable situation. All of their possessions were dry, a good four feet above the floodwater, and they bided their time with Dr. Seuss until the most urgent rescues were made and they could be next.

In Lake April where the Orion terminated, a plethora of death amassed in a surreal apocalyptic scene. Lifeless dogs and cats, cows and horses, and rodents and small mammals blanketed the lake and stacked up like cordwood along the lakeshore. Flies discovered the corpses and a loud buzz filled the air. Garbage and logs and other vegetal debris mixed in with the corpses to form a disgusting toxic waste. And goats, by far the most prevalent of the corpses, started to bloat in the heat of the day.

*   *   *

Sirens echoed along the Rex and Orion Rivers all afternoon as search and rescue operations were in full swing, and Ed Hudson was intricately involved. Only 24 years old, Ed was perhaps the most unlikely person in Darbington to be searching for survivors.

He grew up challenging authority and getting into trouble. He and his buddies took to the streets, throwing food at scrawny security guards, skateboarding through packed restaurant patios, and their favorite, shoplifting beef sticks from an old street vendor.

Ed's parents had several stern talks with him, but the real breakthrough came when they bought him a Nintendo GameCube for Christmas. Ed was soon hooked on it and became a real gamer. He lost interest in prowling through the streets and spent all his free time playing GameCube on his bed in front of his bedroom television. He became quite adept at maneuvering the controller and mastering the video games.

His dexterity was magical, even divine, but it didn't translate to success as a solo guitarist. So now, 15 years after that first game of *Mario Bros.*, Ed puts his dexterity to use operating a drone in the search and rescue unit of the Darbington Fire Department.

Standing on the crest of the south levee of the Orion, Ed hovered his drone over Kidney Bean Island looking for anyone or anything in distress. The red of a car in the remote-control display immediately caught his attention. He clicked on his two-way radio. "ECC, this is Drone Two."

"Go ahead Two."

"ECC, I need a water rescue on Kidney Bean Island. Adult male sitting on a red Prius."

"Copy that. Water rescue on Kidney Bean Island. Adult male on red Prius."

"Affirmative."

"ETA is five minutes."

Ed panned the drone clockwise and couldn't believe his eyes. "And goats! Two of 'em . . . clinging to a cottonwood tree at the east end of the island."

"Copy that. Two goats in a cottonwood tree. Don't see that every day."

"Affirmative."

Five minutes is a long time, long enough for Gordie and Penny to nibble more cottonwood leaves and to snuggle up again to temper the cold. And long enough for Gordie to tell one of his legendary jokes. "It's so cold a dog would stick to a fire hydrant," he bleated.

"What's a fire hydrant?" asked Penny.

Gordie pondered. "I don't know. Something to do with water." Penny didn't laugh or react in any way, but then suddenly she jerked around when the rescuers arrived.

Ed continued searching for survivors, flying the drone downstream along the Orion and scanning on both sides. He came to the concrete flood control weir on the north side and immediately clicked on his two-way radio. "ECC, Drone Two."

"Go ahead Two."

"ECC, I need another water rescue. At the soccer fields by the weir. Two more goats. Can you believe it?"

"Copy that. Another water rescue at the soccer fields. Two more goats."

"Affirmative."

"ETA is four minutes."

Number 21 and Number 44 held onto a floating PVC soccer goal and couldn't let go. Even if they wanted to, they couldn't let go because they were literally hogtied by the goal's net. They floated amongst a sea of orange cones, red referee flags, and multi-colored soccer balls— the flotsam from the many equipment sheds at the soccer fields.

"Ay caramba, I can't move . . . again," bleated Number 44, "and I don't think a tree can save us this time."

Number 21 gnawed on the net. "Try biting the rope. It doesn't bite back like the rope of our humans." They gnawed on the net for a few minutes, but the wound on Number 21's jaw and the toll of the cold prevented them from getting free. And then their ears perked up when the rescuers arrived.

Ed's drone was over the Estes neighborhood of Darbington now. Much of the neighborhood was covered by the floodwater, eliminating the eyesore of blight in hours when, ironically, community leaders couldn't eliminate it in decades. The devastation of flooding was apparent— people wandering the inundated streets in waders and row boats and kayaks, cars and busses submerged, shops and houses and apartments swamped, junk yard dogs barking incessantly from atop piles of twisted rusty cars, a colorful oily film floating on the water in the industrial area, and strange eddies spinning people's missing possessions.

But it was the image of three children rendering aid on the top landing of a playground slide that really struck Ed. Shivering relentlessly just above the floodwater, the kids had covered the victim with their jackets and waived frantically at Ed's buzzing drone. He knew he must act, and act now. "ECC, Drone Two," he radioed hurriedly.

"Go ahead Two."

"ECC, medical response needed. Playground in Larson Park. Corner of Buck and Prater. Three kids helping someone, possibly a parent. Going in for a closer look."

"Standing by."

Ed lowered the drone, and then it nearly fell from the sky. The raven couple, so curious about the strange changes to their habitat after the Ol' Hemhuck dam breach, strafed the strange bird who now shared their altered habitat with them. The collision was violent, with a puff of feathers and an unnatural sputter of the drone motor.

"Fly away!" cawed the male to his mate. "The bird is strong and dangerous."

"Oh shit!" yelled Ed, and if not for those dexterous GameCube fingers the drone would've been in the drink. He steadied the drone and got a closer look, and what he saw was just as surprising as the bird strike. "ECC, I don't believe it! The kids are helping a goat, not a parent. It's goats galore around here!" and with incredulity he started to chuckle.

"Copy that. Three kids and a goat. Medical response at Larson Park. What a day, huh?"

"Affirmative. One hell of a day."

"ETA is three minutes."

Tomás was still quite disoriented from the hypothermia, and the kids' jackets covering him helped only superficially. His eyes fluttered open when Ed's drone buzzed just above his head. *What's that?* he wondered in his delirious state. *A hummingbird? Penny must've been right . . . it was a humming-bird by the sick tree on the hill. I miss my Penny. Where is she? Where am I?* He closed his eyes again, until the blare of a rescuer's bullhorn opened them up.

13

THE DUST SETTLES

April 10

Many heroic tales of rescue and sad accounts of drowning filled the newspapers and online media the day after Ol' Hemhuck burst. Darbington General Hospital was filled too, with patients suffering from broken bones, lacerations, head trauma, and hypothermia.

Three of the patients were found unconscious and draped over a barbed-wire fence, with their clothes and skin shredded by the razor-like barbs. Their loyal border collie dog-paddled to them in the murky floodwater and barked, drawing attention to the dire situation and spawning a rescue. The *Darbington Daily* headlined their rescue as, "The Triple Y Rescue," for each of the rescued men were found hanging upside-down on the barbed-wire fence with their legs splayed and their arms dangling straight down to form the letter "Y."

"You gonna eat that Salisbury steak?" asked Cooper from his hospital bed, the middle "Y" in the Jackson brothers' unique formation. As fate would have it, his was the middle hospital bed too.

Maynard emitted a feeble, "No," his face and lips cut and swollen and almost unrecognizable. He sucked on a box of apple juice, watching a rerun of *Cheers*.

Otis sat up in his bed. "Now wait a minute, I want some more steak. It's the first edible food we've had since we've been here."

"I'll arm wrestle you for it," declared Cooper with a grin.

Otis, with his dominant right arm in a cast, wasn't amused. "Bullshit. I propose you take a look at your gut and then mine and tell me who you think should eat the damn steak."

"Oh go ahead, it's not that good anyway," conceded Cooper to his string bean older brother.

Otis grabbed the plate of Salisbury steak from Maynard's tray, adorned with the omnipresent peas and carrots, and started eating. He talked candidly in between bites. "This flood's gonna set us back a bit. The medical bills are the least of our worries. Getting the business going again could take a while, depending on how many of our goats we're able to roundup. And the house . . . God only knows how bad it is."

"We'll breed what goats we have," stated Maynard, "like in the early days, to get back on our feet again."

"And the house has insurance, right?" added Cooper.

Otis stopped eating and sighed. "Not flood insurance. Whoever thought the fuckin' dam would break?" The brothers looked at each other, and with no words to say they looked at the television just as Norm walked into the bar and all the patrons shouted his name in unison. The brothers cracked a smile, even Maynard whose lips were like sausages, and they felt a little better about things already.

*   *   *

A hastily assembled community flood shelter at Darbington High School quickly filled to capacity. Row after row of made-up cots lined the hardwood floor of the basketball gym, and displaced families and individuals rested on them the best they could under such difficult circumstances. They had mostly sentimental belongings— photos and jewelry and family heirlooms, grabbed in haste before abandoning their flooded homes.

Some kids ran around the gym to release energy, weaving between the cots and brushing by garbage cans that overflowed with fast food boxes and wrappers. Other kids shot hoops at either end of the gym, or they played cards. And two daughters listened attentively to their single mom reading Dr. Seuss, reacting to the book with astonishment and laughter.

The volunteers at the shelter came from all backgrounds including students, teachers, social workers, custodians, car mechanics, doctors, and engineers like Megan Riley. She was remaking a cot when a familiar face approached her apprehensively. Megan couldn't believe her eyes. "What are you doing here? Weren't you high and dry in your mansion by the lake?"

"I wanted to help out," said District Board President Robert Sutton. They want me to sweep the floor. You must be volunteering too."

"Can't beat the commute. I live here now."

"You mean—"

"Yeah, I lost everything."

"I'm so sorry. Listen, I owe you an—"

"No, you owe everyone in the gym an apology! You owe everyone in the fuckin' region an apology!"

Robert bowed his head. "I know, and I know that's not enough. I know the board should have taken you more seriously, but after Cecil Robinson was killed—"

"Save it! I don't want to hear it!" and Megan turned to walk away.

Robert stopped her. "Look, you hate me. I get it. You don't respect me, and that's probably deserved. I'll never make this right, but I want to try the best way I know how."

"What are you talking about?"

"I'm an old man." Robert held out a sealed envelope. "Keep this. You'll know what to do with it when the time's right," and he left for the custodial closet to get a broom.

"The loon," mouthed Megan, and she stuffed the envelope in her back pocket.

Rescued pets and animals, segregated by species, occupied the entire baseball diamond next to the gym. Cats were in cages, dogs were in kennels; and horses, cows, sheep, and goats were enclosed in temporary pens. Distraught pet and livestock owners came by in hopes of finding their beloved creatures. Sometimes they did, sometimes they didn't, and sometimes the shelter residents offered to adopt an animal.

"Mom, I saw some cute kitties outside. Can we get one?" asked the older daughter of the single mom.

"They're someone's pet, dear."

"Not all of 'em. Some of 'em don't have collars. Can we? Please?"

"Yeah, please, please, please, please," added the younger daughter.

The mom sighed and considered the proposition. They did need some joy in their lives, especially now, and besides how could she reject those pleading eyes which had cast such a powerful spell on her. "Well . . . alright."

Pandemonium erupted and they went outside to look at the cats. After an agonizing half hour of looking they had a cat picked out, a playful male tabby without a collar. The mom started filling out the adoption paperwork, but loud bleating from the nearby goat pen distracted her. She stared hard at the goats for a minute, and then finished filling out the paperwork.

"Ma'am, you forgot to sign here," said a woman pointing to the bottom of a paper.

"Oh, sorry. My mind's elsewhere. I can't keep from looking at the goats. It's so funny, some of 'em look so familiar. I swear I know some of the goats." She signed her name, Rosa Rodriguez, and then pulled out her phone to call her older brother Antonio.

PART 6 — WHERE THISTLES GROW

"I'm home and safe and filled with the comfort of being somewhere I've already been. The ruckus of homecoming is brutally enjoyable and everyone makes me feel like a champion. And all I had to do was stay away long enough."

—*Miguel Syjuco, Filipino Author*

14

THE LONG ROAD HOME

After Rosa's phone call, Antonio Rodriguez, little JR's papá, arrived at the community flood shelter early the next morning. He nearly wrenched his back playing *Twister* with Rosa and the girls, and afterwards they sipped on cups of hot chocolate in the cold gym. Antonio peered around the gym at the cramped quarters. "Why don't you come stay with us, until you can move back into your apartment," he said.

Rosa flashed her brother a smile. "That's so nice of you to offer, but we don't want to impose."

"Nonsense! You won't impose, and it'll be fun."

Rosa turned to her daughters, Sara and Eva. "What do you think girls?"

"Can we play with JR?" asked Sara, the youngest.

"Of course you can."

"I want to go," she said.

"Me too," added Eva.

Antonio was ecstatic. "Good! Then it's settled. Now let's go take a look at those goats."

They went outside to the goat pen, a small enclosure housing dozens of goats, and Antonio strained to see if any of the goats were his. "There! That one!" yelled Rosa pointing at a Nubian with mottled tan and white fur and smaller than most of the other goats. "Isn't that Tomás?"

Antonio stared at it for a moment. "I don't think so, it has a bright blue tag on its ear."

"Call it over, see if it reacts to you."

Antonio got right up to the pen and started singing to the goats like he used to do back at the ranch. "The human howls like a dog, but where's his hollow wood?" bleated a Nubian. Slowly it moved his way, then another Nubian, and then a third. They greeted Antonio, two bucks and a doe, by licking his hands through the pen fencing, and Antonio returned the affection by caressing the crowns of their heads.

"Tomás! Gordie! Penny!" exclaimed Antonio. "It is you!" They enjoyed the reunion for a moment and then Antonio frowned. "But what's with the blue ear tags?"

"They can't answer you, Uncle Antonio," snarked Eva.

"You're right. Guess I'll have to get some answers myself."

Antonio walked over to the woman who had taken Rosa's adoption paperwork yesterday, happy but anxious. Happy about finding his precious goats, but anxious about getting them back, especially with bright blue ear tags attached by someone else.

"I'd like to claim three of the goats," he explained to the woman.

"Which ones?"

"Numbers sixty-one, sixty-six, and sixty-seven, with blue ear tags."

"Can you prove they're yours?"

"I have photos of them on my phone . . . without the blue ear tags."

"Without the blue ear tags? That could be a problem."

"But I just gotta get 'em back. They escaped over a week ago. Someone must've found 'em and tagged 'em."

"Hmmm." The woman saw the desperation in Antonio's face and she thought for a moment. "Tell ya what. Give it a week. If no one's claimed your blue tag goats or any of the other blue tag goats, you can have 'em all. Fair enough?"

Antonio had done the math. Twelve goats and 3 sheep had escaped from Rodriguez Ranch the night the coyotes attacked, but only Tomás, Gordie, and Penny were here. The risk of losing them weighed heavily on his heart, but the prospect of getting them back and some replacement goats was appealing. He sighed. "Fair enough."

Later that day Rosa and the girls packed up their few belongings and hopped into the cab of Antonio's pickup truck with their adopted tabby cat meowing wildly in a pet carrier on Rosa's lap. They left the flood shelter for Rodriguez Ranch with smiles all around, the byproduct of relief, gratitude, and excitement.

The next week Antonio made frequent visits to Tomás, Gordie, and Penny at the flood shelter and fed them carrots. Each time he arrived he was so happy to see his goats still there that, in typical fashion, he sang to them. Today it was David Bowie:

"Ground Control to Major Tom, Ground Control to Major Tom . . ."

The week passed slowly, but in the end Tomás, Gordie, Penny, and the other blue tag goats were still at the flood shelter and the Jacksons were still laid up in the hospital, unable to search for their missing goats. Suffering from hospital-acquired pneumonia, the brothers had a tough week with the classic symptoms of cough, nausea, loss of appetite, chest pain, shortness of breath, and fever and chills.

And so, on a wonderful Monday morning Antonio loaded Tomás, Gordie, Penny, and five other blue tag goats into his goat trailer, bound for Rodriguez Ranch. The goats were happy to be leaving the small pen at the flood shelter, but were uncertain of their fate.

"Together we ride the shaking shed again," observed Number 21.

"I'm glad I ride it with you, mi amigo," bleated Tomás.

"Muy bien, you remember the different words I speak! Tell me, did you fight the cold wide water as we did?"

"My fight with it was hard. If not for little humans, I wouldn't be awake."

"We wouldn't be awake either," added Number 44, "if not for humans. They removed the ropes around us and took us out of the cold water."

"Our story is like yours." bleated Penny. "We held onto a tree until humans took us out of the cold water."

"I don't understand humans," started Tomás. "They can be good and take us out of cold water, and they can give us first meal." He turned to Number 51, the Savanna who lost his brother to Cooper's knife. "But they can be bad too, don't you think?"

"Very bad," agreed Number 51. "A human made my brother leak red and not wake up."

"I know the human who shakes this shed is good," continued Tomás.

"How can you be so sure?" asked Number 51.

"He howled like a dog and fed us carrots where we last ate grass."

"So."

"So, the human is good. And think about this shaking shed. It's not too crowded like in the other shaking sheds before. It's comfortable, and I think where the human takes us will be too."

"I hope you're right," bleated Number 51, and they bounced around in the trailer for several minutes until suddenly the shaking stopped. After over two weeks away from home, dealing with the tragic deaths or disappearances of nine goat comrades, and surviving their own near-death ordeals; Tomás, Gordie, and Penny were home.

15

NO PLACE LIKE HOME

Tomás, Gordie, and Penny weren't the only ones to return home, the Jackson brothers came home from the hospital after recovering from pneumonia. The floodwater had receded to reveal a muddy home that was uninhabitable for most, but the Jacksons were not most. They rounded up wooden pallets without nails poking out, cleaned them off, and arranged them into three platforms— one for sleeping, one for garbage and human waste, and one for food and drink. "That'll do," said Otis of their platforms, "home sweet home."

Despite still recovering from their flood injuries, they got right to work cleaning up their three-bedroom ranch house. They made a huge pile of ruined possessions by the toppled goat barn, consisting of carpet, furniture, clothing, books, mattresses, appliances, and 10 years of accumulated knick-knacks.

However, some of their possessions could be saved. The brothers painstakingly removed drawers and doors from furniture, cleaned all the pieces with soapy water, and dried them for hours with a fan on high before reassembling the pieces. They handwashed clothing twice to remove silt and clay, then hung it up on a clothesline to dry. Special knick-knacks, like the fish trophy Cooper earned in a bass tournament, were cleaned and placed with the restored furniture and the laundered clothing on a fourth wooden pallet platform for salvaged goods.

Maynard cleaned an old kettle barbecue at the end of their hard day of work. He lit some charcoal briquettes, and once they glowed red he tossed six burgers onto the grill. "Good job today boys," said Otis over the sizzle of meat.

Cooper dipped into an ice chest. "Here," he said, and he threw Maynard and Otis a cold beer. Maynard held a spatula in his right hand and Otis' right arm still had a cast, so both of their left-handed catches were pretty amazing, or perhaps just lucky. They tipped back their beers.

"Did you know we're still gettin' mail?" said Otis. "Checked it today. The damn box is filthy as sin, but the mailman still delivers it."

Cooper sat atop the ice chest, his own beer in hand. "Neither rain nor snow nor an apple a day keeps the—"

"Hold it right there Coop, you fucked it up," said Maynard from the grill.

"Whatever. The point is the mailman always delivers."

"And do you know what he delivered today?" The broad smile on Otis' face tantalized his brothers.

"What?" they asked eagerly.

"Seems we got a letter from the bureaucrats saying that they're gonna pay us in full even though we didn't finish the levee work, and what we did finish got wiped out. We should get a check by the end of the week."

"Alrighty then," said Maynard.

"Cha-ching!" shouted Cooper.

The burgers were ready and Maynard brought them over to Otis and Cooper. Everyone sat on their butts on the food and drink platform with full plates and another round of cold beers, eating without talking. And then the silence was broken. "What the hell is that?" said Maynard with only burger dregs and smeared ketchup remaining on his plate. The brothers squinted at an animal in the distance.

"Let's go see," said Otis, and they put their plates down and their rubber boots on. Surprisingly the animal didn't flee as they traversed the muddy ground and approached it. They got closer and could see that it was an exhausted goat, gaunt and covered with mud. Only feet away, Otis could read the number on its bright blue ear tag. "Holy shit, it's Number Four. He's one of ours. We're back in business boys!"

*   *   *

Megan left her temporary home at the community flood shelter when her friend and neighbor Trish invited her to come stay with her. Trish, whose house also was flooded, was staying at her Aunt Dorothy's house in an unaffected neighborhood of Darbington. Megan continued to work for Ol' Hemhuck Water District, where a lot of Monday morning quarterbacking was going on, and to volunteer at the flood shelter which wasn't nearly as crowded as before.

The smell of burnt toast and coffee filled Aunt Dorothy's kitchen. Megan and Trish scraped and buttered their pieces of toast while Aunt Dorothy slathered peanut butter on hers. Everyone crunched toast and sipped hot coffee, and Aunt Dorothy picked up the crossword puzzle in the *Darbington Daily* and pondered.

"How's it goin' Aunt Dorothy?" asked Trish.

"Twelve across . . . roller coaster feature . . . second letter is an 'o'."

The women thought for a moment, and then Trish shouted out "loop!"

"Ah yes that fits, thanks dear. I'm not very good at these. That's enough for now." Aunt Dorothy flipped the newspaper to the front page and started reading.

Megan turned to Trish. "Want to take a bike ride this weekend?"

"Sure. Where to?"

"I hear the Waldorf Trail is nice. It snakes through the wine country."

"We might just have to do a little wine tasting."

"Oh, that's so tragic," said Aunt Dorothy.

Trish looked at her aunt with a blank face. "Excuse me?"

"Oh, not the wine tasting . . . the old geezer." She pointed to a story in the newspaper. "Says he mixed up his meds and died . . . so tragic. Guy by the name of Robert Sutton."

Megan's jaw dropped, and so did her mug of coffee onto the floor. "What a klutz I am . . . let me get that." She carefully picked up the broken mug and blotted spilled coffee with a wad of paper towels. "Excuse me," she said after dumping the mess in the garbage can, "I'll be back in a few minutes."

"Is everything alright?" asked Trish.

"Yes . . . of course. Finish your breakfast and I'll be right back."

Megan retreated to her bedroom and searched frantically for the sealed envelope Robert had given her at the flood shelter. She finally found it after rifling through a large stack of her work papers, tore it open, and extracted a single piece of paper and read. It took a minute for the magnitude of its contents to sink in. *Crazy bastard,* she thought, and then she called the phone number at the top of the paper.

"Shuster and Hodges," the man on the line said.

"Uh yes, I'm holding a copy of Robert Sutton's will. I thought I better call you."

"Just a minute please."

After a solid five minutes the man came back on the line. "Are you Megan Riley?"

"Yes."

"We've been expecting your call. Robert provided your name as executor of his will. His untimely death is just so tragic."

"Yes, so tragic. Being executor, what does that entail?"

"You'll administer his final wishes, and as you probably already know, that's to bequeath his entire estate to the victims of our recent flood."

"Yes, of course." The man confirmed the unbelievable that she suspected. "How generous. How will the victims receive his assets?"

"His liquid assets will be distributed based on need to some two-thousand uninsured renters and homeowners in the region, many of them in the Estes neighborhood. Later, after his house and other property are liquidated, those assets will be distributed based on need also. That's a total of about nine point two million dollars."

"Nine point two million dollars! Wow, this is a lot to take in."

"We're here to help you through the process in any way we can. Don't be a stranger."

"I won't be."

"Is there anything else I can help you with?"

Megan pondered for a moment. "Yes, did Robert have a family? Any others in his life?"

"He had a divorced wife, but she passed away years ago."

"I see. Well, thank you. I'll be in touch. Bye."

A flood of emotions shook Megan like a quake— rage for Robert's ignorance, sympathy for the guilt he must have felt, gratitude for his generosity, sorrow for the loneliness he may have experienced, and grief for his passing. *Crazy bastard,* she thought again. *Thank you crazy bastard, and rest in peace.*

*   *   *

It didn't take long for Tomás, Gordie, and Penny to become reacquainted with Rodriguez Ranch. Rogue still faithfully patrolled the pasture, and sheep still grazed the fescue and avoided the spray of the impulse sprinklers. But the sheep, which numbered 15 after the coyote attack, had no interest in eating star thistle and in the absence of the goats it proliferated. The biggest adjustment for Tomás, Gordie, and Penny was the heartache of not having many of their goat friends at the ranch anymore, but they were glad to have the five new Jackson goats.

"I missed eating the sharp plant that grows here," bleated Penny with a mouthful of star thistle.

"Plenty for everyone," added Tomás. The cut on his cheek had healed nicely and he chewed without pain. He turned to the Jackson goats. "Do you like it?"

"It's quite good," bleated Number 29, an elderly Boer.

"We ate this a lot after we rode the shaking shed to the weeds," added Number 39, another Boer.

"Makes me thirsty," bleated the Savanna Number 51.

"Our water's in the shed," added Penny, "and the humans keep it clean."

Spanish goats Number 21 and Number 44 joined in the feast, and Gordie welcomed them as only Gordie could. "Hola mis amigos, want to hear a joke?" He misunderstood their silence for a "yes." "Alright then, what do you get when you sit down in a field in Spain?" More silence. "Gracias."

Number 21 and Number 44 wagged their tails, not in approval but merely by coincidence, for the joke had escaped them. "No need to thank me," bleated Number 21, and he started to eat again. He ate another 15 minutes and then gave his sore jaw a rest and laid down to ruminate. Some other goats laid down by Number 21 to ruminate too, and a chorus of burps filled the air.

The goats regurgitated their cuds back into their mouths for a second round of chewing and swallowing. "Ah, second meal," bleated Number 29.

"We call it segunda comida," added Number 44.

Some grazing sheep had worked their way close to the ruminating goats and could hear the conversation. "Where I come from we call it the twain meal," bleated a Suffolk ewe."

"Don't listen to that big piece of cotton!" yelled Gordie.

"How rude you are! I'll never understand your kind," bleated the ewe, and the grazing sheep moved on.

"Do they always follow each other like that?" asked Number 51.

"Always," replied Tomás, "but they're not so bad. Dogs are bad, as I'm sure you know."

"I know all about dogs, they—"

The conversation ended abruptly when JR, Sara, and Eva sprinted through the pasture and scattered all the goats and sheep. JR touched Sara. "Tag, you're it!" he shouted, and Sara started chasing Eva and JR. They ran around for 10 minutes until exhaustion set in. The ever-watchful Mamá brought them cold glasses of lemonade while Papá went over by the goats.

"Ready dear," yelled Papá and Mamá came over. "Alright, first order of business is to lose the number," Papá told Tomás. He held out an apple slice that Tomás promptly devoured, and then put him in a headlock while Mamá quickly popped out his bright blue ear tag with an ear tag remover. "Goodbye sixty-six!" yelled Papá, "and welcome back Tomás!"

Mamá and Papá caressed the crown of Tomás' head. "That wasn't so bad," he bleated. "Nothing like when the other humans poked me there." The other goats stood around, more curious than alarmed, and Papá lured in the next goat for a headlock with another apple slice.

Seven more tags they removed and two more names they restored, Penny and Gordie, but five goats remained nameless and for Mamá and Papá that just couldn't be. "Okay kids, want to help us pick out some names for the goats?" asked Mamá. The excited kids bounced around like Superballs on concrete.

"Me first!" shouted JR.

"No me!" shouted Sara.

Eva tried reason. "I'm the oldest. I think I should go first."

"We'll do it together," said Mamá. "Do you think you can do that?"

"Yes," the kids replied, and when their brains engaged the bouncing around subsided. When it was over a half hour later, Mamá and Papá were exhausted but the goats had names— Number 21 was now Santa, Number 29 became Bubbles, Number 39 was Candy, Number 44 was Buttercup, and Number 51 was Tarzan.

The sheep and goats worked the pasture the rest of the day, mowing down the fescue and star thistle and the other invasive weeds and plants that grew so rampantly in the spring. They ruminated without interruption, safe from the kids who were napping in the house after all the excitement of the day.

At dusk Papá wheeled a large bag of grain in a wheelbarrow down to the pasture, happy to have eight more mouths to feed. "Come 'n get it," he shouted as he walked along the white wooden fence pouring grain into the attached wooden trough. And come they did, like a herd of angry elephants.

"What's all the commotion?" asked Buttercup.

"Yeah, what's goin' on?" bleated Bubbles. "We never did this at our home."

"It's feeding time!" yelled Gordie.

"Ya gotta get in there. Follow me!" shouted Tomás, and he showed the Jackson goats all of his mealtime skills to ward off those angry elephants— stomping, spinning, shoving, and headbutting.

"Say . . . this is good," bleated Candy between bites.

"Más . . . necesito . . . más," bleated Santa who proceeded to vacuum up all he could.

"I'm thirsty," stated Tarzan after getting his fill.

"Come with me," bleated Penny. "We'll get some water."

After the feeding the goats and sheep went to rest in the A-frame shed and under its porch. Stomachs rumbled with Papá's offering, and Rogue patrolled the quiet pasture beneath the faint glow of a crescent moon.

"I must show you something," bleated Gordie to his new goat friends. "Over there, do you see the animals with white eyes running one way and the animals with red eyes running the other way?" His friends nodded. "They've made us leak red and not wake up. Stay away from them. They're dangerous. They're big and fast and make scary growling noises. I think they must be the makings of humans."

"We've seen them before," bleated Tarzan, "where we eat weeds by the wide water. The danger isn't in the makings of humans, it's in the humans themselves. As I've told you, my brother leaked red and didn't wake up at the hand of a human."

"Maybe we're both right," bleated Gordie, and he regurgitated, chewed, and swallowed Papá's meal again. "Well, that's it for me. Goodnight everyone." He closed his eyes for a few moments but then suddenly opened them up, for his night was about to change for the better.

Papá desperately wanted to start milk production again, and that meant mating his does. He knew all about the affinity Tomás and Penny had for each other, and after observing the new goats sensed that the Spanish goats Santa and Buttercup would be a good pairing. That left pairing bucks Tarzan and Gordie with does Bubbles and Candy.

"What's goin' on?" bleated Gordie to Papá. "I'm tryin' to sleep here." But Papá would have none of it, slipped a rope around Gordie's neck, and slowly led him to an empty stall in the back of the A-frame shed. Next came Bubbles who was equally baffled.

"Okay guys, let's take care of business," said Papá, and he left the stall to get Tarzan and Candy.

"Why'd the human bring us here?" wondered Bubbles.

"I don't know," replied Gordie, "but it's nice here. The air seems warmer and the ground's covered with dry grass. Let's lie down."

The goats settled comfortably onto the straw together, and the scent of their pheromones quickly filled the stall. Though Gordie wasn't rutting, instinctively he asked, "Want to have a go at it?"

Bubbles, who wasn't in heat replied, "I like you and I think you're funny, but I just don't feel like it."

"Oh. Maybe when you do feel like it."

"Absolutely. Besides being funny, you're kinda cute." Gordie wagged his tail, but not for long, the noise of Tarzan arriving in the adjacent stall distracted him. "Won't you tell me a joke?" asked Bubbles.

The question immediately brought Gordie's attention back to his girl and his face lit up. "Of course," he replied. "I've never been asked that before. Let's see . . ." Gordie tried to think of a joke but was caught off guard, so instead he nuzzled his head into Bubble's white fur and he licked and nibbled on her big floppy ears.

"Never mind," she bleated. "I don't need to hear a joke. I have everything I need right now." They stayed nuzzled through the night, until some unexpected visitors stopped by at dawn.

"Wake up!" shouted Tomás. The other goats were with him, some dangling star thistle from their mouths after a quick bite of breakfast. "I was just standing on a rock smelling the wonderful asparagus and carrots in the air. We're gonna walk through the white wood . . . not to escape dogs, but to feast! Won't you come with us?"

Gordie and Bubbles jumped to their feet, more from the surprise of the visitors than the excitement of the pending adventure. "Of course," bleated Gordie. "We wouldn't miss it."

The goats walked quietly to the pasture gate beneath the last of the fading stars. Tomás put his front hooves on the middle rail of the gate, like he did during the coyote attack, and raised his face to the top of the gate. He carefully poked and jostled the metal latch with his nose and, without the duress of attacking coyotes, it clicked open on the first try. Tomás pushed hard with his front legs, but being a small Nubian the gate only creaked open slowly.

An ominous figure moved not 10 feet away, obscured by the cloak of dawn's sparse light, giving Tomás and the other goats quite a scare. It was a gaunt and exhausted and muddy goat, like Number 4 who had miraculously returned to the Jacksons. "Who's there?" demanded Tomás. The figure got closer. "Rocky? Is that you? What are you doing here?"

"I came back," he bleated. His eyes were tired and his voice was weak. "I'm sorry for the things I said about you."

"Don't worry about it. That can be expected on a hard journey like ours."

"I know you were just trying to lead us the best you could. And now I know just how hard it is to lead." Rocky cast his eyes downward, and Tomás was hesitant to ask his next question.

"Where are the others?" he bleated. Rocky shook his head. "I see. May those who don't wake up be happy."

"May they be happy," repeated Rocky. He paused to listen. "I don't hear the mean dogs, why do you walk through the white wood?"

"To feast on asparagus and carrots. Won't you come, my friend?"

"Of course, I need to get some meat back on my bones."

"Great to have you back, Rocky!" Tomás reared up playfully on his hind legs to butt heads with him in the dance of the goats. Rocky reared up too, and then they cocked their heads, paused for a second to stare down each other, dropped their front legs to the ground, and rammed their hornless heads together.

"Nice one, Tomás!"

"Nice one, Rocky!"

The goats clippety-clopped down the asphalt driveway at Rodriguez Ranch. Tomás put his nose in the air to get his bearings, and then they turned left onto the private asphalt road serving the Rodriguez's house and four others. They stopped at the first house on the road, the one with the large raised-bed garden. "The asparagus and carrots are just over there," bleated Tomás. "Let us feast!"

The sun was up now, lighting the green and brown and orange of the garden. A light breeze rippled stems and leaves. Morning birds fluttered about, singing to the world below. For the goats of Rodriguez Ranch, it was the start of a perfect day. Just perfect. The first perfect day of many more to come.

Also by Bruce Shaffer

The Man with the Yellowfin Tuna
It Started with a Pickle Crock
The Bonnacon Goes to Calgary
The Bonnacon Goes to Pamplona
The Final Play
The Folsom Rewind